WHY DID THEY KILL?

These were nice kids, model kids. They didn't wear leather jackets and roam the streets in "wolf packs"; they didn't steal and mug for dope. For kids, they were well mannered and quiet. They were attractive and nicely dressed. You'd have welcomed them as next-door neighbors.

Yet...

one raped

one murdered

one killed by fire

What got into them? What dark thoughts tormented them when they were alone at night?

The Twisted Ones

Vin Packer

PROLOGUE BOOKS

F+W Media, Inc.

Published in electronic format by
PROLOGUE BOOKS
an imprint of F+W Media, Inc.
10151 Carver Road
Blue Ash, Ohio 45242
www.prologuebooks.com

eISBN 10: 1-4405-3700-3
eISBN 13: 978-1-4405-3700-4

POD ISBN 10: 1-4405-5614-8
POD ISBN 13: 978-1-4405-5614-2

This is a work of fiction. Names, characters, corporations, institutions,
organizations, events, or locales in this novel are either the product of the author's
imagination or, if real, used fictitiously. The resemblance of any character to actual
persons (living or dead) is entirely coincidental.

This work has been previously published in print format by:
Gold Medal Books / Fawcett Publications, Inc., Greenwich, CT.

PART ONE

Chapter One

BROCK BROWN

It was perfect. They were both watching him. Dr. Mannerheim from the window of his classroom on the third floor, and Carrie Bates from the rear of the school parking lot. Brock could see *her* out of the corner of his eye as he turned his key in the ignition. She was leaning against Derby Wylie's old Ford. She was laughing too loudly, with her shining black hair spilling to her shoulders, and the front of her shaking under one of those long, heavy-knit sweaters all the girls at High wore this year. Brock pressed in his radio "On" button and waited for it to warm up. He did not look up at the window where Mannerheim stood smoking his pipe, but he could feel Mannerheim's eyes on him. Okay, head-shrinker, he thought, make something out of this scene.

One of the boys was giving Carrie a light. To the right of the group assembled there, a couple was doing the fish. She began singing—not words but "Oooh, ew, ew, beedely ah dop ew," coming on that way, and clapping her hands in rhythm. Moving like she did. Supposed to be sexy or something.

When his radio was tuned in, Brock turned it way up. "Send Me Crazy," blared. Brock waited a second. He could see the shadow of Mannerheim's figure above him, without looking up at him, and he knew Carrie was only pretending to ignore him. She was snapping her fingers now and Derby Wylie was shouting "Go" with her beat.

Then Brock stepped on the gas pedal and pressed the horn. He backed out so fast that his wheels squealed when he stopped to shift, and when he went forward, the gravel spun and nicked the fenders of his Chevy. A cloud of smoke poured from his exhaust, and he went down the drive like hell. He looked in the rear view mirror. He could see the figure of Mannerheim vaguely, but he would have to adjust it to see her. He was too cool to play it that dumb, to let either one of them see him fixing the mirror, so he just drove on, imagining the picture they both got of him leaving school that afternoon. Sunglasses. Top down. Music playing. Going like crazy . . . Brock Brown, boy cat, all shook up.

He was a tall boy with a good build, and a better wardrobe than most guys in the junior class at Sykes High, thanks to his stepmother. He had a handsome face with big dark eyes that were both quiet and wild in their expression. His hair was black and thick, and he liked to wear it cropped close on top, with slight sideburns to the tips of his ears. He dressed meticulously, with a rigid sense of style that he had formulated over the years. Dark against light—that was the core of it; never more than two colors at a time, even in his socks. Today he had on a navy blue flannel shirt and navy trousers, with a white belt, a white nylon zipper-jacket, white wool socks, and white shoes with white rubber heels. It had not been easy to find the shoes. Most of the doeskins had red rubber heels. Brock had searched and searched, and finally he had convinced his stepmother to drive him to Syracuse, twenty-six miles away, and there he had found the kind he wanted.

Brock had not made a fraternity. Carrie Bates was in a sorority; in fact, she was president of the Tri Gams. That was one of the reasons it was hard for him to come on with her. She was always on—with anyone. Every time Brock saw her, Carrie was walking with some guy, grinning up at him with her eyes sparkling; or standing by his locker, touching his sweater with her fingers, or touching his wrist, or a book he was carrying. She had very long nails that tapered to a point, and were always painted the color of blood. Afternoons at Murray's Luncheonette, where the crowd hung out, the table where Carrie always sat—the one right up front by the jukebox—was always surrounded. It was like she held court there or something,

Brock decided. Maybe he really hated her. Maybe he couldn't stand her or something.

He was torn between two impulses as he drove away from Sykes High on Grant Avenue. One was to head toward Murray's. The other to go on home. He knew that if he went to Murray's, he'd only sit up at the fountain by himself nursing a coke and smoking a cigarette, pretending he wasn't interested in one damn thing going on in the crummy place. After awhile she'd come in with Derby Wylie and the others, and the minute she did, he'd make a point of crushing out his cigarette very emphatically, tossing a dime on the counter, and striding out past her without so much as a glance at her. That was one way of handling it. . . .

Another way was to wait until she sat down at the table. Then he'd get off the stool, walk over to the jukebox, and play H-9. It was classical—the only one on the whole goddam machine that was, and that ought to tell her something about what he thought of her. She was all rock 'n' roll and do the fish and come on with anyone in pants, and that ought to shake her up. Then he'd walk back to the counter, take a swallow of coke until he caught her eye, and just when he did, he'd let his mouth tip in a vague, sardonic grin, pull up the collar on his white nylon zipper-jacket, and exit—bang, crazy!

Why the hell hadn't he tuned in on something classical before he'd cut out back at the school parking lot! Why hadn't he thought of that? There ought to be something high class on the goddam radio. He began to push the buttons in to try and find something. When he couldn't, he turned the car radio down, and slowed up. He decided on the lazier impulse—to go on home.

Dr. Mannerheim was a smart cat. Brock wondered what Mannerheim thought of him. Brock was flunking his course, but hell, he *knew* the stuff! He knew what Mannerheim was driving at. Psychology was very damn fascinating, but learning it for Brock was like trying to remember a name, or a familiar face, or something that had happened a long time ago. It was there, but Brock couldn't get at it. It was like trying to remember last night's dream. There was that peculiar sensation that you'd participated in something, felt something, said and listened to something, but what was it? It was crazy and evasive, that's all.

The whole hour Brock sat in Mannerheim's class, he had the feeling that in just a second the goddam clouds would part, and he'd see everything as clearly as day, and then he'd know—know everything Mannerheim was trying to get across; but it never quite happened. Why was that?

Sometimes Brock had the idea that Mannerheim was talking only to Brock during the hour; that Mannerheim was trying his best to get something across to Brock. Whenever that happened, Brock would smile and nod, or purse his lips and frown solemnly, as though the message was clear and he understood it. To impress Mannerheim, Brock often checked out very pedantic books on psychology from the school library. After class he'd take one of them up to Mannerheim's desk and point to a sentence.

"I wonder if you could clarify this, sir," he would say.

He was very careful to say "sir," and to be sure his hands were scrubbed clean. They were rarely dirty, but on days when he would do this, he would scrub them until they were red just before his psych hour.

Once Mannerheim said to Brock, "I didn't know you were so interested in psychology."

"Yes, sir, I am," said Brock.

"Don't you think you ought to master the assigned textbook before you do outside reading?" Mannerheim said.

That had really cut.

Brock wouldn't look at Mannerheim for about five days after that. Then he forgave him. He didn't exactly forgive him. He simply decided Mannerheim was right. If Mannerheim didn't know how to spot a phony by now, what kind of a head-shrinker was he, for Christ's sake? The experience made Brock respect Mannerheim more.

One day Brock would have a talk with Dr. Mannerheim. He'd like to get his opinion on a few things. Not bad things he'd ever done; he'd really never done bad things. His attitude toward Carrie Bates was proof of that, wasn't it? He didn't give two cents for any of that crowd, or whatever the hell they did on their goddam dates, and he could just imagine. Brock was more mature. He'd like to get Mannerheim's opinions on some psychological questions that had nothing to do with sex.

It was almost hot, for a day in early May, in upstate New York. Brock played with the idea of pulling over and slipping off his jacket. A lot of guys would have tried to take off their jacket while they were driving and maybe killed someone in the deal. But Brock wasn't that kind. He hated to think of anyone being hurt. Sometimes when he read those books about what the Nazis had done to Jewish women during the war, he actually felt like bawling. He was never able to get the tears out, and it was terrible—like being constipated or something. After he read one of those books he'd rip and pull at it in blind rage, and then he'd pray. Not *for* anything. He would say long prayers of thanks. Thanks for his car, his eyesight, his clothes, his hearing—thanks for everything.

Brock drove along debating whether or not to succumb to the heat and remove his jacket. Who the hell would see him between here and home that he cared about? Besides, his car was white, and he'd still look good wearing the navy blue shirt against the car's colors. But the collar of the shirt did not stand up the way his jacket collar did. . . . He decided he could bear the heat.

Maybe on his way home, he'd drive past the Bates place. He knew Carrie's mother to speak to, because he'd had a paper route when he was a kid, and Friday nights when he collected, Mrs. Bates always paid him personally. He had an idea she rather liked him. He had an idea that she felt sorry about his mother dying. Mrs. Bates and his mother had been friends, as girls, way before his mother had ever married Robert Brown. "Brock" was his mother's maiden name. One thing he could always remember was his mother saying, "You're a Brock, son. Don't ever forget that. The Browns weren't anything, but the Brocks were The Ones in Sykes."

Brock always believed that Mrs. Bates thought of him as one of The Ones, and he usually tried to behave humbly before her, as though he was aware of it but not in any way conceited.

He imagined that if he drove by the Bates', and Mrs. Bates saw him, and they were to wave at one another, no doubt she'd say to Carrie that night: "Brock Brown drove by this afternoon. He's such a nice boy."

That ought to show Carrie Bates.

Brock glanced at his watch, whipping his arm up smartly to do it—a quick flip of the wrist like that, and then back on the wheel. He gunned the car a little, as though he had noticed it was very late for some appointment he had, and he must hurry. He looked in the rear view mirror, but actually there was no one around to see him that he cared about. He felt suddenly depressed and sleepy.

He wasn't late for anywhere, but it was three forty-five. If he went directly home, instead of going by the Bates', his father could have the car to go to work. It was Brock's car, but he liked to lend it to his dad. He had a piece of tarpaulin in the back, so that his father didn't get grease on the slipcovers. He felt sorry for his father sometimes. He wasn't embarrassed by him or anything like that. Hadn't he stopped in at the garage time and time again and called out: "Hi, dad!" for anyone to see? It was just that it was too bad that happened to be what his father did. He ran a goddam garage, that's all, and a man who did that always looked dirty.

His father was a great guy, and Brock was even glad that he'd married Clara. Clara couldn't help the way she was. Sometimes, though, Brock wished she would act her age. Sure, she was younger than his dad, but she was twenty-seven, for Christ's sake, and Brock wished she'd cut out all the lovey-dovey stuff. Poise was what Clara lacked. Mrs. Bates had it, and Brock's mother had had it, but Clara came on like she thought she was Marilyn Monroe sometimes. There was another thing about Clara Brock didn't like. If he didn't have such a good grip on himself, Clara could sure screw him up, pow! whamo!— in-no time. He knew she only did it because she thought he needed self-confidence—he knew *that* much about psychology—but if he hadn't known that, he might have gotten all sorts of crazy ideas from Clara. Only last night, for example; last night right smack in the middle of the Ed Sullivan Show.

"Brock?"

"What, Clara?"

"Are you going to the prom?"

"I don't know, Clara."

"Why don't you ask Carrie Bates to the prom?"

"Are you crazy?"

"You're always talking about her. Why don't you ask her to the prom?"

"Do you know anything at all about Carrie Bates, Clara? Anything at all?"

"I've seen her. She's very pretty."

"Oh sure, pretty. Pretty. But do you know anything about her?"

"What do I need to know about her?"

"Do you realize you could get me in a whole big crazy pack of trouble if I didn't know right from wrong, Clara?"

"What are you talking about, Brock?"

"I'm talking about Carrie Bates."

"Go on."

"Well, nothing. Nothing. Except she's fast. Whizz! Bang!"

"Brock!" Clara laughed. "Are you afraid to ask her? Afraid she'll turn you down?"

"Now listen, Clara, I'm telling you she's fast! She's fast! F-A-S-T! Do I have to spell it out for you?"

"All right, Brock. All right."

"You just better get the facts, Clara, before you make a suggestion like that."

"Okay, Brock. Okay."

"I mean, Jay-Zeus, Clara, you just better know what you're talking about."

"Okay, honey, forget it. It was just a suggestion."

"Some suggestion!"

"Brock?"

"Huh?"

"Do you know you're beautiful?"

"Clare-ra!"

"I mean it, Brock. You can have anything or anyone you want in this world. Look! You belong in the movies!"

"I know. Brock Hudson, boy movie star."

"You mustn't tear yourself down all the time."

"What do you want from me, Clara? I'm trying to watch Ed Sullivan, and you come on this way."

"I just want you to be happy, Brock."

"So? I'm happy."

"You ought to go out more. Make friends, that's all, Brock. You're a very attractive young man. Remember that."

"You remind me from time to time, Clara. Promise?"

Brock Brown had never had a date with any girl. Last year when the new English teacher had asked all the students to write a short biography at the beginning of the Fall term, Brock had started his with the sentence: "At fifteen, I, Brock Brown, boy cat and all shook up, have had no sexual experience."

His father and Clara had been summoned to the principal's office and confronted with the essay. He would never have known about it if his father had not taken him aside one night and said: "Look, son, about that composition you wrote at school. Go easy, fellow. Sex is a four-letter word in Sykes."

"I was being funny, dad."

"I know you were."

"Besides, it's true, dad. I mean, I was being funny, but it also happens to be true. Plenty of guys my age can't say the same."

"All right, Brock, but Clara's worried. She thinks you might have sex on the mind. Do you, son?"

"Oh, crazy! Clara's some cat to talk!"

"What do you mean by that?"

"I'm not the one with sex on the brain, dad. That's all."

"And Clara?"

"Nothing, nothing, nothing. The whole thing's a big wild joke, for the love of Pete! If I'd thought there was going to be this much stink about it—"

"All right, son. We'll just forget it. But don't tell Clara I mentioned this to you."

His stepmother's reaction to the affair was to buy Brock a new sport jacket and to say, "You're the most attractive young man in Sykes, Brock."

"Thank you, Clara."

"Don't you worry."

"Worry?"

"You're all right, Brock—in every way."

Brock lived in a yellow stucco house on Marvin Avenue, right off East Genesee. It was a nice neighborhood. Sykes, New York, was funny that way. There really wasn't such a thing as a bad neighborhood. Of course, there were those few tenement houses down on Clancy Street by the dam, where the Negro people lived, but over-all, no matter where you lived in Sykes, there were people of all kinds on your street. Even on Marvin Avenue there were Jews. The Rubins on the corner. Mrs. Rubin was a small, thin, flaxen-haired woman with a good shape and a rather flashy way about her. Sometimes in the summer she hung around the yard in shorts and a halter, and whenever Brock went by in the car and saw her like that, he always said a special prayer of thanks that no goddam Nazi had ever gotten his filthy hands on Mrs. Rubin, and made her get naked, and done cruel things to her. He didn't even know Mrs. Rubin, but he felt very deeply about *that*. Why couldn't men stop being so goddam violent in the world? Why!

Pulling up to the curb in front of his house, Brock was pleased that he had decided to come here, instead of chasing off to Murray's. His father deserved the car. His poor, unhappy father. Working in a garage the way he did; having his wife die on him; and then winding up with Clara, and her lovey-dovey act. It was sad. Really sad. Brock put out his cigarette in the ashtray on the dashboard, and sighed with a melancholy air.

But in the home to which Brock was returning, there was no consciousness of anything sad or melancholy. Mr. Robert Brown, at the age of forty-two had never felt happier or more successful in his life. In another year, he would own the Blue Star Garage. He was making enough to keep his new wife happy and eventually to send his son through college. His marriage to Edith Brock had been a dismal failure, and sometimes it seemed as though God himself had intervened in favor of Robert Brown and taken Edith to the grave, where at last she would rest in peace. Edith had been everything Clara wasn't—cold, puritanical, superior, never able to forget her family had money once; a hateful, sharp-tongued termagant who treated her own son as the intruder she felt he was. Robert Brown was glad Brock couldn't remember his mother well. She had died when he was seven, and Robert Brown decided it was one of life's ironies that Edith's life had been lost in childbirth, a birth she did not want to give and didn't give, but took the unwanted boy to the grave with her this time.

Brock Brown's father was the best mechanic in Kantogee County, never mind Sykes, and Clara was a woman who made a man glad just to be alive. He—unhappy? Coming from anyone, the idea would have floored him.

Coming from Brock, it would have shocked him. When Edith was alive, Robert Brown's main concern had been Brock's welfare. Edith did not have it in her to love the boy, nor even to feign some semblance of affection or approval where Brock was concerned. She could barely stand to lift him up and hold him in her arms when he was a baby, nor to change him—particularly to change him. She hated him to "soil"—her word—and after he learned to walk, whenever he dirtied himself, Edith could not control her temper.

"*You* like dirt," she would shout at Robert Brown, "you wallow in it! But I detest it!"

Robert Brown was no match for Edith Brock. He had none of her polish, nor any education beyond high school. After her father drank away the Brock fortune, Edith at thirty-two was a left-over spinster, working at the bank, and periodically driving in to the Blue Star Garage for repairs on her Studebaker. Robert Brown, age twenty-six, was a shy, impressionable young man who never dreamed how desperate Edith Brock was, nor how susceptible to pity he was. He married her feeling sorry for her, and she married him feeling exactly as he did.

Fate, God, Chance—whatever it was that had abruptly terminated their marriage, Robert Brown owed his happiness to it. He waited one year, a proper amount of time, and then he began to drop into Crowell's Department Store, where Clara Lewis worked. She was fifteen years younger than he was, and she was a war widow. The competition was manifest, but Robert Brown persisted. Five years from the time he first took her to a drive-in movie, Clara married him.

Brock's father never thought he was doing anything but the right thing. He knew it was the right thing. Clara was young enough to understand a growing boy, and old enough to enter a second marriage with a mature woman's desire to work at making it a success. To *work* at it? Robert Brown laughed when he thought of that word. He might have had to work at any marriage with Edith, but Clara and he were naturals. It was more like play. It was the best thing that had ever happened to him, next to having Brock.

His wife's feelings paralleled his own. Clara loved Robert Brown so much she wanted to cry sometimes at how perfect it was between them. She loved Brock too, and he made her want to cry as well, but not out of happiness— more out of frustration. That kid was such a swell kid— so darn good-looking and nice, and he didn't seem to realize it. You could tell him until you were blue in the face, but it simply didn't register. What do you do for a kid like that? Clara had bought him clothes, got Bob to buy him a used car, and even tried to talk him into dating girls, but nothing seemed to help. Brock was Brock—that was the only way to look at it. Oh, he was sarcastic sometimes; sometimes he was a little cocky, but Clara never minded that. In a way it reminded her of Alan—what she could remember of Alan. They'd only been married a short time before he'd been shipped over, and then killed, but there was a lot of Alan in Brock. Remember how Alan used to love nice clothes too? Clara would pick out ties and socks for him, the way she did for Brock. Yes, Alan was a real clothes horse. Sharp, he used to say. That's a sharp tie. That's a sharp suit. That was the word. Times changed. Brock always said "crazy" or "smooth". He was the cool one, all right. Aw, poor Brock. If she could only help him. Not be his mother, or anything dumb like that. She was only twelve years older than he was. But help him. That was what she wanted to do—help Brock.

Neither Clara Brown nor Robert saw Brock pull up in front of the house that afternoon. He usually went to Murray's after school, or drove around for awhile before he came home. It was unusual for Brock to arrive as early as ten minutes to four. Robert Brown was due at the garage at four. His night man was sick this week, and Brock's father was taking his shift.

He had pulled Clara down beside him on the sofa in the living room. She was kissing him while he smoked a last cigarette before he started for the bus, and he was pretending he wasn't in the least affected by what she was doing.

"What are you going to do tonight while I'm gone?" said he.

"Watch television."

"That all?"

"Miss you."

"Somebody's licking my ear," he said. "Did you let a cat into the place?"

"I don't know who could be licking your ear. Who'd want to lick your ear?"

"I don't know," he said. "Who'd want to do *this* to you?"

"Rob-*bert* Brown!"

"Do you know anyone who would?"

"Now, you just *stop* that?"

"What?"

"That! Feels too good."

"Don't go getting hot on me now."

"You're asking for it."

"You getting hot on me?"

"Am I ever!"

"Maybe I'll catch the four-thirty."

"Maybe."

"Well, what do you think?"

"I love the smell of your clothes, Bob! Oh God, I love the smell of your clothes."

"Baby, I can get the four-thirty just as easy."

Brock had been standing in the hallway for the last two minutes. He had looked around the corner and seen Clara lying on top of his father. Seen her wiggling that way, and seen his father's hand up under her clothes. He had jumped back, and he stood there rigidly, rubbing his knuckles with the palm of his hand, biting his lip and thinking how nasty they were. His father in his grease-daubed coveralls; his father's hands so ingrained with filth that even Borax applied with a scrub brush could not make them clean, so that the lines there were black, and there was black under his nails. His father with a slut like Clara, letting her come on that way. Jesus Christ, Jesus Christ, Jesus Christ! How could a guy grow up clean in his own house, keep himself clean around people like this?

Brock tiptoed back out the door, letting the screen close noiselessly, the way he'd come in. He walked toward his car and got in. He sat there. Soon he'd have a headache. He leaned forward and let both elbows rest on the circular chrome that made the horn blast. He let it blast a few seconds. Then he straightened up and got out again. He went down the walk slowly this time, whistling. It was beginning in his head. Always in the same place. The pain was like a bandeau that fit in a line across the top, from one ear to the other. It wasn't too bad; it wouldn't be for a while.

He opened the screen door and shouted out, "Hey, cats!"

"Brock?" His father's voice. From the living room.

He sauntered in, grinning. They were sitting side by side on the couch.

"I brought you the car," said Brock. "Thought you'd like to take it to work."

"Thanks, son. That was nice of you."

Clara said, "Hello, Brock."

"Hi."

"Well," said his father, "there's no time like the present." He got up. There was some change, and keys, and a package of cigarettes on the coffee table. Robert Brown stuffed them into the pockets of his coveralls. "Did you have a good day, Brock?"

"Crazy!" said Brock. "Don't forget the tarpaulin for the front seat, dad."

"I can take the bus, Brock. I don't mind it."

"I want you to have the car," said Brock. "That's why I came home."

His father said, "I appreciate that, son."

After his father had left, Brock followed Clara out to the kitchen.

"Clara," he said, "I'm in sort of a jam."

He could feel the headache getting worse.

"What kind of a jam, dear?"

"I bet a guy ten dollars, and I lost."

"Not again, Brock!"

"I thought sure I'd win this time."

"Aw, Brock, you mustn't gamble. You mustn't."

"I know that. I know that now. You won't tell dad."

"I never have, have I?"

"The guy's waiting for me at Murray's, Clara."

"I'm not made of money, Brock," she said, but she laughed, and Brock knew she would give it to him.

At four-thirty, Brock got off the bus at Houston Street. Houston was a quiet, residential street, but it was near the downtown business section in Sykes, and there were cars lining the sides. His headache was so bad now that every step he took seemed to jar him, making the pain more intense. He knew how to walk along past the cars and look inside without seeming to. He would never do this at night; he wasn't that sort, not a sneak. Besides, he only had a Junior Operator's license, and he was not suppose to drive after dark. That was the law.

At the end of Houston, near Stewart Street, he found one. It was a green Mercury. The windows were down, and

he saw the key. With a practiced nonchalance, he opened
the door. He lit a cigarette before he got in. Way down at
the end of the street, two women were headed in his direction. He made no effort to hurry. He settled himself
behind the wheel, moving the seat forward, adjusting it
to his height. Then he started the motor. His headache
was at its peak.

He pulled out of the space carefully. He knew lots of
guys who didn't care how they pulled out; didn't care
whether or not they scraped someone's fenders or hit
some poor jaywalker. Brock wasn't that thoughtless. He
went down Houston slowly and shifted at the stop sign
by Stewart.

He drove for a long time. Not fast. About forty. He
had the radio on softly, but he didn't listen to it. He felt
his headache and he talked to it.

"You don't want to hurt me," he said, "I know that. I
understand. Can't you go yet? Can't you?"

He was somewhere outside the city limits, up near the
lake. There were a lot of back dirt roads in this area, and
he picked one out and went on that. "It's all right," he
said to his headache. "It's going to be all right."

He went for miles over the hard dirt, thinking that it
hadn't rained in too long, thinking that he wished it
would rain and he could let it rain on his head, how cool
it would feel, good.

His headache was beginning to stop. Brock slowed up.
He drove the car up into the ditch and cut the motor. He
sighed and sat back with his eyes shut. Not for very long
—a minute, two. When he opened his eyes, the headache
was gone.

From his pocket, Brock took out the ten-dollar bill
that Clara had given him. With a rubber band, he at-
tached it to the gear shift. There was no one anywhere
in sight out here in the country, but he whispered anyway. He always whispered when he said a prayer.

"Dear God, thank you," he said, "for my health, for my
home, for keeping me strong and clean, for everything
you've done for me. Thank you and amen."

Brock got out of the Mercury. He gave the door a gen-
tle pat, as if to say: "You'll be all right."

Then he walked down the dirt road in the direction of
the highway. He never minded hitching a ride back to
town. After all, it was only fair.

Chapter Two

CHARLES BERREY

Some 208 miles away, in another small city, that same afternoon, the Berrey family was preparing for a big evening. Charles Berrey, the unexpected fruit of Howard and Evelyn Berrey's middle age, was to make his third appearance on Cash-Answer, the most popular quiz show on television.

Charles was eight, and he had already won $33,000. He was small for his age, and incredibly nearsighted, but he was a darling-looking youngster with tea-colored hair and a good sturdy build; bright blue wide-laughing eyes that were usually hid behind whirls of prescription-ground glass, and an endearing smile made more so by the fact that his upper left bicuspid was missing.

His ears were being cleaned that afternoon by his mother, in the kitchen of the small Berrey bungalow, and it was a happy moment for both mother and son.

"I reiterate," Charles was saying, "you're hurting me."

"You *what?* You *iterate*?" his mother giggled.

"I reiterate," said Charles, "I *repeat.*"

"My little Chuckles," said Evelyn Berrey proudly. "My little genius."

"Don't call me by that infantile name," said Charles Berrey, "I simply abhor it!"

"Oh, you do, do you? You abhor it, do you; little Mr. Iterate."

She tweaked his right ear, and he squealed delightedly.

Evelyn Berrey watched with pride-swollen eyes, marveling again at the fact this boy was hers. Him, with an I.Q. of 165, standing up before all America like he'd done last week, rattling off the kings of Israel and Judah as easily as if he were saying his ABC's.

"Saul was the first king, son of Kish. Ish-Bosheth, son of Saul. David, son of Jesse. Solomon, son of David. Rehoboam, son of Solomon. Uzziah, son of. . . ."

On and on, naming them off that way, until Jackie Paul, the quizmaster, shouted out, "You get cash for your

answers, because your answers are cor-*rect!*" Then the
drums beat, and the bells rung, and the light above
Chuckles in the Contemplation Chamber blinked on and
off, and the audience went wild. Mrs. Berrey had been
moved to tears.

What made a boy like Chuckles know all that, Evelyn
Berrey wondered? It was his memory. It was photograph
or something. Evelyn Berrey herself had a perfectly rotten
memory. God, when she thought about it, it was a wonder she remembered her own name, and the same for
Howard. All Howard remembered was ball scores. Howie,
Jr., too. He was just like his father—all baseball games
and fix-things-down-in-the-basement, and Marines this
and that. He was handsome in his uniform, all right,
Howie was, and he used to be terrible thoughtful, sending
home those pillows with MOTHER in gold on them, from
Parris Island, but he'd grown away since he married that
I-talian girl. It had beat Evelyn why Howie ever picked
an *I*-talian for a wife. The years certainly changed things.
Howie living down there in West Virginia with an *I*-tal-
ian, not even coming East for Christmas last year; and
Chuckles all grown up and winning a fortune on the tele-
vision.

Mrs. Berrey tweaked his left ear and said, "If you don't
hold still, Mr. Cash-Answer, I'm going to tell Jackie Paul
your name is Chuckles. Ha, how'd you like that!"

"If you do . . . if you do," said Charles Berrey, "I'll—
I'll—"

"Ah? What? What'll you do if I tell Jackie that, ah?"

"I'll pulverize you," said her son.

Mrs. Berrey bent double laughing. This kid could come
up with the darnedest thing! "You'll what? Ah?"

"I reiterate," said Charles Berrey, "I'll pulverize you,
mater!"

In the living room of the Berrey household, Howard
Berrey ground out his cigarette and tossed his copy of
Baseball Annual on the table. He got up and paced
around the room, back and forth in front of the imita-
tion fireplace, a huge bull of a man with a build like a
boxer. He was proud of his figure; proud of the fact he
kept in shape. You wouldn't catch old Duke Berrey getting soft, or growing an extra feed-basket. He was in the
same shape he'd been when he'd played tackle out at old

M.U., and he could still run the mile without fighting for breath. He worked out at Harvey's gym here in Reddton, New Jersey, every other night, and when he was on the road, he worked out at a "Y." It wasn't simply a matter of vanity either; it was good business. A man who sold sports equipment around the country couldn't expect to gain any respect from a customer if he wasn't in tiptop condition himself. Hell, Duke Berrey was in a lot better condition than nine out of ten of the college coaches he ran into. He could demonstrate anything he sold from a leap tick to a punching bag, without looking silly, and that was a damn important part of sales—to show the customer you used the product yourself.

Duke Berrey wasn't going back on the road until this television ordeal was over. He had mixed emotions about Chuck's success. He was glad the kid was winning all that money—that part was great. Not that any kid of Duke Berrey's had to go on a quiz show to earn money for college, but it was a real boon just the same. By the time Chuck was ready for college, Duke might feel like taking it easier, slowing up a little. A man deserved to slow up when he reached his fifties. But the part Duke didn't like was people's reaction to his kid. People thought his kid was some kind of freak or something. After the last show, one of the men in Howard Berrey's company had walked up to him and said, "Tell me something, Berrey. How the hell do you talk to your boy? I mean, what the hell do you talk about?"

"He's no different from any kid of yours," Howard Berrey had answered. "He's just got a good memory."

"Yeah, yeah, Berrey, but he had to read all that stuff first, to memorize it. Kid of mine can't even read the funny papers."

Duke had no answer for that. It was true that Chuck read books like a hungry tomcat devoured mice; read anything he could get his hands on, and when he ran out of things, Chuck hiked himself off to the library. Sometimes he came back with as many as ten books, the absolute maximum he could check out. History books, books on geology, novels, books on art—hell, anything that was between covers.

What'd he want to do all that reading for?

It was probably Evelyn's fault, though the good Lord knows when Duke Berrey met Evelyn, she didn't know

Paris was in France. It had to be Evelyn's fault. All the while Howie Jr. was growing up, Duke had been home. He hadn't accepted the sales job until after Howie enlisted in the Marines, and look at Howie. You couldn't find a better kid. Howie'd read a book or two himself, but they weren't his East and West, for Pete's sake. Even if Chuck was bright, Duke wouldn't worry if he wanted to be an engineer or something; if he wanted to read up on something that would help him careerwise in the future, but what kind of a job was Chuck going to be able to get when it came time? Some kind of teacher? Some kind of professor? Make beans for a salary?

Anyway, Duke Berrey wasn't going to worry about Chuck's distant future that afternoon. There was the immediate future to ponder. There was tonight. Chuck was supposed to be at the studio by eight-thirty. Evelyn and Duke and Chuck were having dinner in New York with Duke's boss.

"I'd like to meet that boy of yours," Mr. Carter had said, "Do you think that's possible, Duke?"

Duke Berrey had tremendous respect for Paul Carter. Here was a man who'd started at scratch, worked himself up the ladder one rung at a time until now he was president of Sterling Sporting Goods. No college degree, no fancy-pancy; just a hell of a lot of damn hard work and a love of sports. It was a pleasure to work for a man like Paul Carter, and more than anything, Duke Berrey hoped the respect was mutual.

For a moment longer, he listened to Evelyn and Chuck giggle and babble in the kitchen, listened until he was sick and tired of it, and then strode through the hallway out there and stood in the entranceway, glaring.

Charles Berrey looked up at him with a puzzled expression. He was never able to fathom his father's moods. He liked his father much better than he liked his mother, but he knew that when it came to their feelings for him, it was the other way around.

His mother said, "Well, what's eating you?"

"Let's all play a game," said his father, "Let's all try to talk in words of *one* syllable for twenty-four hours."

That was funny. Charles Berrey had to laugh at that one. Maybe if he got the chance, he'd tell that one to Jackie Paul tonight. It was good irony, under the circumstances, he decided.

His mother said, "I'm afraid that's the only choice *you* and *I* have, Howard."

Charles Berrey watched his father's expression. Was he angry at something? It was very difficult to decipher any meaning from his father's expressions.

"Chuck," said his father, "do you remember who we're meeting for dinner?"

"That's a hot one," his mother said. "Does he *remember.*"

"Mr. Carter," said Chuck. "President of Sterling Sporting Goods."

"The boss, to *you*," said his father.

"The boss," said Chuck giggling. He liked his father. His father was most amusing.

"Has Carter got any kids?" his mother asked.

"Three."

"Oh yeah? I never heard anything about them."

"Well, they haven't been on television, if that's what you mean, Evelyn."

"I'll bet they haven't," said his mother.

"What are you trying to say, that Paul Carter's kids aren't any good because they haven't won any money on Cash-Answer? Is that your theory, Evelyn?"

"That's only one of my theories. I've got a lot of theories about Paul Carter."

"Like?"

"Like how come he suddenly wants us all to have dinner in New York? Hah? How come all of a sudden old man Carter wants us all to come in and sit around at dinner with him, Howard?"

"He wants to meet Chuck."

"Oh, sure. Sure. Just wants to meet Chuck," said Evelyn Berrey. "He's had eight years to meet Chuck, and twenty-two years to meet Howie, and he's never got around to either before now."

Charles Berrey was pleased. What his mother was saying was true. Mr. Carter had asked them to dinner because of him. Charles Berrey was pleased because he had done something for his father. It was never easy to do anything for dad; in fact, when before had he ever done *one* thing that dad really approved of? You see, the difficulty was one of basic communication between himself and his father. They had enormous trouble exchanging ideas. It was perplexing.

"Shut your yap, Evelyn," said Howard Berrey. "Just shut your yap!"

"Maybe Carter would like Chuck to plug Sterling, hah? Just a little plug, hah?"

"Evelyn, Carter's just taking an interest in Chuck," said Howard Berrey, "and I'm damn honored."

"Oh, honored. Honored! He's got three kids of his own to take an interest in, hasn't he? But he's big-hearted, Carter is. Old big-hearted Carter. Going to ride to Glory on Chuckles' coattails."

"Shut up, Evelyn. I'm warning you!"

"His own kids are flops. Flops!"

"At least they don't wet their beds every night," said Howard Berrey.

That was the last thing he had wanted to say. He stood in helpless silence while his son ran from the room. He stood sick inside of himself, hating his own guts, not even caring that Evelyn Berrey, opposite him, was calling him the biggest goddam bastard of all time.

At five-thirty that afternoon, Charles Berrey heard his mother say: "Well, you've got to go in and talk to him, Howard. That's all there is to it."

Charles was sitting in his room on the bed, with the door shut, but in the Berrey house, the walls were so thin you could hear right through them.

He had been reading Ironside's book, *British Painting Since 1939*, but he quickly pushed it under his pillow. He hopped off his bed and went across to his knife rack. His father had begun Charles Berrey's knife collection last Christmas by presenting him with a standard hunter's knife and a Japanese sword. For his birthday, his father had given him an Indonesian knife with a guarded blade, which Charles learned was for rice-cutting. His brother Howie had sent him a straight-bladed knife used by the Temme in Africa for sacrifice. While he was not very enthusiastic about this collection, Charles had learned to feign fascination. Best of all, Charles liked the little chipped flint knife he had bought with his allowance from the Musuem of Natural History. It was the kind used in the Neolithic period, and it did not look as frightening or dangerous as the rest.

When his father came into the room, Charles Berrey was

pretending to examine one of the knives, as though he had been absorbed in this occupation all along.

His father said, "Hi, fella!"

"Oh, hi, dad."

"I thought we could have a little confab, Chuck."

"Sure, dad," said Charles Berrey. "I was just looking over my cutlery."

His father sighed. "You always find another way to say it, don't you, Chuck?"

"Knives are cutlery, dad."

"*Table* knives, Chuck. People don't call other knives cutlery."

"On the contrary," said Charles Berrey, "all knives are cutlery. Why, the cutlass was named for that purpose. That was a sword used by sailors on war vessels."

"Chuck, I didn't come here to argue with you."

"I wasn't arguing, dad."

"It beats me why you just can't say knives. Why do you have to show off and say cutlery? People say knives. And people say ships, not vessels. Did you ever hear a sailor say he had to get back to the *vessel?*"

"No, sir," said Charles Berrey pushing his glasses back on the end of his nose. "No, sir."

"Now you're mad, I suppose."

"No, sir, I'm not angry."

"Chuck, is it so hard for you to say the same things ev-everyone else says? I just said 'mad.' You said 'angry.' Now would it have killed you to say, I'm not *mad.*"

"No, sir."

"Chuck, don't *sir* me, son. I mean, why does everything have to get so formal between us?"

"I don't mean it to, dad."

"I know you don't, Chuck. Oh, God, I don't know." His father sank down on the bed and cracked his knuckles. "Chuck," he said, "I came in here to tell you I was sorry for saying that back in the kitchen."

"It's all right, dad. I didn't mean to have such severe reaction."

His father sighed again, staring at his large hands, while Charles Berrey pulled his chair out from his desk and sat on it.

"Did I say something wrong again?" said Charles.

"You don't say anything wrong, Chuck. It isn't that

you say anything *wrong*, for Pete's sake. Look, Chuck," his father said, "I'll try to demonstrate something. In my business, one demonstration is worth a thousand words. Now, look . . ." His father thought for a moment. Then he stood up. "Chuck," he said, "Come over here and punch me. Punch me right smack in the belly as hard as you can!"

The boy regarded him momentarily with a puzzled frown. He got off the chair and walked across to the father. With his fist raised, he paused questioningly.

"Go ahead, Chuck! Sock me right in the belly, hard!"

Charles Berrey did as he was told.

His father winced. "Ow!" he said, "That hurt!"

"I'm sorry, dad."

"No, now—wait a minute. I said, that hurt! It hurt, Chuck. Do you get that? Now, if I hadn't expected it, and you'd just walked up and pounded on me that way, it might make me mad. Do you understand, Chuck?"

"I think so, sir."

"So I'd be mad at you, see? And if you were to come to me later and apologize to me, I'd say: 'Well, Chuck, I didn't mean to get so mad.' Do you see, Chuck?"

"Y-yes, I think so."

"In other words, son, I wouldn't go into all that stuff about severe reaction. I'd just plain say right out that it had made me mad."

"Yes, dad."

"Okay, Chuck?"

"Yes. Okay."

"That's all there is to it, Chuck," said his father smiling. "You just say what you mean."

"I see," said Charles Berrey.

His father sat back down on the bed, more relaxed now. He said, "How do you like being in the limelight, kid?"

"All right."

"You know, Chuck, your mother and I are damn proud of you."

"Thank you, sir . . . dad."

"Now, it was your decision to go on again this week, right?"

"Yes."

"And you'll make it, kid. I'm not at all worried about *that*."

"What are you worried about, dad?"

"Worried? Well, Chuck, I'm not *worried*. You can't call it being worried. I just want to have a chat with you."

"All right, dad."

"For instance, tonight. Jackie Paul's going to ask you a few questions before you go into the Contemplation Chamber, right?"

"Yes, sir. I mean, *right!*"

"Oh, you know—routine questions. What do you do for a hobby. What are you going to be when you grow up. That kind of stuff."

Charles Berrey giggled. "I guess it's pretty plain what I do for a hobby."

"You mean read, Chuck?"

"Sure," Charles laughed.

"Well, now, Chuck, you weren't reading when I came in. You were playing with your knife collection, weren't you?"

"Yes, dad."

"Why don't you say something about your knife collection? I bet Jackie Paul doesn't even know you have one. Or any of the people watching television. They must think you're all books."

"I see," said Charles Berrey.

"I'm not telling you what to say, Chuck, but people already know you read a lot. People already know that."

"Yes, sir."

"And remember when you were a kid you used to want to be a ball player. Remember that?"

"Sort of," said Charles Berrey.

"You mean you don't remember that? Remember how we used to throw 'em out in the back yard? You and me and Howie?"

"Yes, I do, dad."

"Well, tell 'em that, kid. I mean, you have a lot of sides to you. You're no darn bookworn, for Pete's sake, Chuck."

"All right, dad."

"I don't want you to get the idea I'm trying to influence you, son, but you want to make a good impression."

"I see."

"Okay?"

"Sure, dad."

"That's what counts, Chuck—the impression you make."

"All right."

"Good!" said his father. He stood up and reached out to ruffle Charles' hair. Charles Berrey backed into his knife rack and jumped away in a sudden motion, as though he had been burned.

"What's the trouble?" said his father.

"Nothing."

"That knife rack's secure." His father said. He walked across and patted the sides of the rack. "That knife rack's okay, Chuck."

"I *know* it is."

"You jumped like one of those knives was going to pop out and fall on you."

"They *could* fall," said Charles.

"Fall out of there?" his father chuckled. "Now, come on. How could those knives fall out of there? They're held tight."

"I guess they simply make me anxious now and then."

"You mean they *bother* you now and then?"

"That's right," said the boy, "they bother me."

"Well, don't worry about it, kid," his father said.

"I won't, sir."

"One more thing, Chuck."

"Yes?"

"Tonight when we meet Mr. Carter . . . Tell you what, Chuck, let's spoof him a little. Want to?"

"Spoof him?"

His father laughed. "That's right, spoof him a little, Chuck. Let's tell him you got a B on your last report card."

"B in what, dad?"

"Oh, anything. I mean, let's just say you got a B. He'll think you got all A's, you know? I mean, you *did* get all A's, but let's spoof him."

"Tell him I got a B?"

"Say you got a B in English or something. English! That'd spoof him. Say you got a B in English."

"That's my best subject, dad."

"They're all your best subject, for Pete's sake," said his father. "You never got a B in your life, did you?"

"No, sir. Never."

"So say you got one, Chuck. In English. I mean, that's irony, you know? You with your big words, you know *irony?*"

"Yes, sir."

"Well, wouldn't it be ironical if you were to get a B in English?"

"Yes, sir. I suppose it would."

"Mr. Carter must think you're all books and good marks, and it'd spoof him if you told him you actually got a B."

"Yes, sir. Dad. I guess it would."

"Want to do that, Chuck?"

"Sure," said Charles Berrey. "I want to do it."

"Thatta boy!"

"What about mom, though?"

"I'll fix mom, don't worry. She'll play along. I'll fix her!"

The boy hesitated as his father opened the door of his room.

Then he said, "Dad?"

"What, kid?"

"When you fix it with mom, dad. I mean, you won't terrorize her?"

"I won't *what?*"

"Nothing."

"Terrorize, for Pete's sake? Terrorize!"

"I mean, make her mad. That's all."

"Where do you get a word like terrorize?" said his father.

"I meant make her mad, dad."

"You've got to learn to say things the way other people say them," said his father, "You've just got to, Chuck."

"I'm trying, dad. I'm making every effort."

"Oh, Chuck, for Pete's sake! Every effort!"

"I'm trying, dad," said the boy, "I meant to say I'm trying."

"Well, don't go and bawl on me!"

"I *won't!*"

"And don't shout, Chuck."

"I'm sorry. I apolog—I'm sorry, dad."

"Okay, kid. Let's just forget it. Okay?"

"Yes, sir," said the boy. "Yes, okay, dad, sir."

"Okay," said his father, "Okay, kid," and he shut the door behind him.

Charles Berrey stood alone, his glasses steamed up, and behind them, his eyes were filled with tears that began gradually to slide down his cheeks. He wiped them away angrily with the palms of his hands. He was bawling, just the way his father said not to; crying like some kind of baby; and even worse, he had wet his pants again.

Chapter Three

REGINALD WHITTIER

"That would make it exactly fourteen days after my period," Laura Lee told the boy, "I might not even have been ovulating."

It was the same day and the exact hour that Brock Brown was getting into the green Mercury in Sykes, New York, and Charles Berrey's ears were being cleaned by his mother in Reddton, New Jersey.

This was taking place in New England, in a small Vermont town famous for insurance companies and Red Clover Junior College. The setting was in complete contradiction to the conversation taking place between the slim, solemn nineteen-year-old boy and the short eighteen-year-old girl with the close-cropped, wind-blown, sun-colored hair. Auburn, Vermont, was a town typical of the state— sedate, unexciting and plain. And Whittier's Wheel, the antique shop where the pair was holding this conversation, was as archaic and old-fangled in its appearance as the attitudes and opinions of its proprieteress, Miss Ella.

Miss Ella was the mother of the slim, solemn nineteen-year-old boy, but no one in the whole of Auburn or its surrounding county would think of calling her Mrs. Ella, nor even Mrs. Whittier. Who could, and who would want to remember back to the year when big, coarse, whiskey-ridden Theobald Bruce had seduced this fragile lady and put a life in her? He had married her and given her son a name, under the duress of the townspeoples' angry threats, and for the same reason he had run off to Canada, never to be heard from since. Miss Ella did not bother to use the Bruce name, nor to allow her son to use it, but proudly called him by Whittier, called him by Reginald, the name of her father.

She was Miss Ella to everyone, a dear sickly soul whose

courage in remaining there in Auburn, despite the chance
of gossip and criticism, was remembered long after the in-
cident with Theobald Bruce was. People in Auburn remembered what they wanted to, forgot the unpleasant and
mean, went about their business and prayed in church for
things to stay the same.

On the wall of Whittier's Wheel, right above Reggie
Whittier's head, was one of his mother's samplers, with
the words stitched in lavender against a yellow back-
ground:

"If you can't be a pine on the top of the hill,
Be a scrub in the valley—but be
The best little scrub by the side of the rill;
Be a bush if you can't be a tree."

It would have come as a near-fatal shock to Miss Ella
to know that it was this sampler which had ignited the
spark responsible for the few moments of sudden fire between her son and a maid from Red Clover Junior College. The truth was that Reginald Whittier II did not
want to be the best of whatever he was. He was, in fact,
bent on being better than what he was. His experience
with Laura Lee had not helped, but his determination
in the matter was unique.

"I don't know whether I was ovulating or not," said
Laura Lee, "You can't really tell unless you take your temperature for a whole year."

There it was—*more* mystery. Reggie Whittier decided
there would never be an end to the mystery of woman; no
matter how much he had read and been told, he would
never know everything. He was, at the same time he realized this, vaguely uncertain that he wanted to know everything, and he pictured a thermometer in his mind, and
thought of the way his mother always had one sitting in
a glass of water beside her bed.

Reggie had been told the facts of life when he was sixteen years old. His mother had asked Mr. Danker, the
town jeweler, to explain everything to him, and Reggie
had sat in hot discomfort, listening, while his mother did
her needlework across the room. Mr. Danker described
everything in his precise, pontifical tone, and Reggie
was torn between not wanting his mother present at this
time and not wanting to be alone with Miles Danker while
he discussed the subject.

It was not that he disliked the paunchy, balding jeweler. There was no one in the whole of Auburn who knew as much as Mr. Danker knew about everything, nor was there anyone as kind to Reginald Whittier as Danker was. But whenever the boy was alone with him, Reggie felt extremely nervous and at a loss for words. Reggie supposed it was because he was not accustomed to the company of men. Women were much easier for him to communicate with. Not girls—except for Laura Lee, who was both a fluke and a godsend—but older women like his mother, the kind of women who came to Whittier's Wheel to look at antiques. Reggie could talk to them for hours on end about nothing at all.

Yet for all Miles Danker had told Reggie, and despite the fact that Reggie had read up on women in a book Laura had lent him, he felt that the female sex was the most mysterious thing in the whole world—felt that even now, after he had been with Laura Lee. Laura lived in a trailer on the outskirts of Auburn with her mother and father, who also worked at Red Clover. Miss Ella called them itinerant workers, because in the summer the Lees went to Florida to work in a hotel. They were no different than migrant workers, said Miss Ella, and she referred to the trailer camp as "Tobacco Road."

"It isn't that I object to you keeping company with a lady, Reginald," she told him, "but that girl is not a lady. No doubt she has diseases. Ask Mr. Danker what kind."

Reggie had no intention of asking Mr. Danker about it. Every time he remembered that session with Danker when he was sixteen, Reggie felt immensely guilty and depressed. There was really no reason for him to have that reaction, but there it was, and Reggie suspected his mother felt exactly as he did.

She once said, "I would not have put us through that horrible experience, Reginald, if I had not felt that it was absolutely necessary. There are certain sordid things in life one just has to face."

Laura Lee had told Reginald Whittier something similar, only she had put it this way: "It's never easy, Reg. Life don't make it easy, but God made men and women different for a purpose. We're supposed to."

She had said that immediately after their sudden experience in the Lee trailer, that night Mr. and Mrs. Lee were down at the Green Mountain Movie House. Laura was trying to make him feel better about what had happened between them. It was the first time for both of them, and both of them had wanted it to happen. But afterward, neither one felt the least bit glad or wise.

"I suppose," said Laura, "it's because we weren't really in love."

"I never knew a girl like you," Reggie said. "I could never talk to a girl before you."

"Yes, but it's not like love. We're supposed to be thrilled or something."

"I know it," said Reggie.

"I'll tell you one thing, Reggie Whittier. You're the only boy I've ever wanted to do it with. You were never fresh and you never tried to maul me. You're the nicest boy I know."

"I really have a feeling for you," said Reggie.

But nothing either one could say that night at the end of April could change the fact that both were sorry the thing had happened. Reggie always thought of it that way—as "the thing." He had expected it to be so different. He had thought he would feel like a conquerer, feel the way he had seen the men in the movies behave. He remembered one movie in particular. The scene had faded on a man and a woman as they embraced, and then in the next scene, after time had elapsed, the man was dressing, tying his necktie and slicking back his hair with military brushes, grinning and whistling as though he had just inherited a hundred million dollars.

Reggie had felt like two cents.

"Well, what if I *am* pregnant?" said Laura Lee that afternoon in May as she faced him in Whittier's Wheel.

"Shhh, Laur, please. Don't shout."

"I don't want to shout, Reg."

"I know you don't. I'm sorry."

"But what if I am?" she whispered.

"I'll—I'll marry you," he said.

"Oh, Reg, you know we can't get married. How can we get married? My father'd *kill* me!"

"So would my mother," said Reggie. Then he changed his mind. "No," he said, "It'd kill her."

"*Why* did we do it?"

"It was a dumb thing," Reggie said.

"I don't hold it against you, Reg. You know that."

"Sure, Laur. It was my fault."

"It wasn't anyone's fault, and that's the truth," she said, and then, "Do you think I'm pregnant?"

"Listen, Laura," said Reggie, looking over his shoulder, back toward the stairs in the shop which led up to the apartment where he lived with his mother. "It makes me nervous to talk about it here. I'll get the car tonight. Can you get off early?"

"At ten-thirty."

"I'll pick you up," he said.

"What about your mother?"

"It'll be all right."

That was a lie, and Reginald Whittier knew it. Every Sunday his mother clipped out the television section from the *Times* and circled in red all the evening programs they were to watch together.

"It isn't that I mind your going out," she would tell him, "but I did buy the television for you, after all. Don't you remember our decision, Reginald? We decided that it would be less embarrassing for you if you were to enjoy entertainment in your own home. You know how it used to embarrass you to go to the movies alone? I don't blame you one bit, either. I've always hated going anywhere alone, but I'm an old woman, and I'm content to stay home now. I bought the set for you, dear."

His mother had bought the television before he met Laura. In most ways, his mother understood him very well. Reggie was shy around anyone his own age, except for Laura—shy and slow and clumsy, but the worst part of all was that he stuttered. He was never sorry that he had not gone on to college, nor that he was declared unfit for military service, and that was the reason. In high school, he was a nonentity. You read novels and see television shows and hear all the time that stutterers are poked fun at, and mocked, and mimicked, but in Auburn High, Reggie was simply ignored. He was Miss Ella's son. He helped her out in the Wheel. He was a jerk. That was all there was to it, and sometimes Reggie was not even sure he was thought to be a jerk, because most of the time he believed he simply wasn't thought about at all by anyone.

When Laura came into his life last September, there was a radical change.

She had come up to him in Stoker's Drugs on the cor-

ner, where he went for malts during one of the afternoon "breaks" which his mother allowed.

The girls from Auburn barely nodded to him, and the
girls who went to Red Clover never looked at him. He
never minded the fact that the Red Clover girls payed no
attention to him, but he *had* gone to school with most of
the Auburn girls. When they slighted him, Reggie felt
more and more determined not to show his face anywhere.

"It's only because you stutter," his mother would tell
him. "You're a perfectly nice boy, but if they spoke to you,
you'd have to answer back, wouldn't you, Reginald? And
you'd stutter. They're only trying to save you embarrass-
ment."

Laura Lee was different. She had come up to him in
Stoker's and handed him her shoe. The heel was broken,
she explained, and would he run across to the repair shop
with it while she waited for him? She told him her name
and smiled at him. It was something that could have
happened to anyone, without the moment meaning anything at all, but it had happened to Reginald Whittier.

He had never known a warmer feeling than the one he
had as he crossed Lowell Street with her shoe. He felt as
though he had taken some sort of dreamy dope, or as
though he were slightly intoxicated. He stood before Mr.
Canzetti with his shoulders squared and a broad smile on
his face, and he told an utterly preposterous lie. "Mr. Canzetti, my girl friend broke her heel. Can you fix it up?"

"Well now," said the old man, "you got yourself a girl
friend, huh, Reginald?"

"Why not?" Reggie answered.

He stood whistling and waiting while Mr. Canzetti
banged on the shoe, and it was peculiar that he remembered again the man in the movie, tying his necktie and
slicking back his hair with the military brushes.

When he walked back to Stoker's and handed her the
shoe with its heel repaired, she said: "Want to have a
coke with me, or are you busy?"

"I wh-wh-wh —"

"You *want* to," she said.

"Yes."

She said, "My brother stutters. He's a mechanic down
in Sarasota."

To Reggie, it was just as though she were saying: "My
brother has brown eyes."

He could almost feel tears start. That was another embarrassing thing. Reggie Whittier's eyes always filled with tears over the least little thing. He seemed always to be on the verge of crying. But never because of anything sad —only because of things that were simple and happy. Once a week he cried when he watched This Is Your Life on television. Whenever they brought someone out of the subject's past for an unexpected reunion, Reggie would sit with his eyes full. He cried at movies, and he cried if it was a sunny day and his mother said: "Aren't we happy, though? Aren't we lucky we've got all our limbs and our senses, Reginald?" He cried when Perry Como sang "The Lord's Prayer"; and sometimes when one of the boys or girls he had gone to high school with *did* wave at him, he felt like crying.

His mother understood. "It's not because you're a sissy or anything at all like that, though most people would be the first to say it was. It's just that you're an extremely sensitive boy. That's another reason I bought the television. You have a right to feel the way you do."

After that initial meeting with Laura Lee, he saw her three or four times before she came to Whittier's Wheel to seek him out. He saw her in Stoker's, and on the corner of Clover Hill in her denim uniform, waiting for the bus to take her up to college, and he saw her once in Mc-Govern's Department Store. He would wave at her and smile, but not until she came to the antique shop did he have his second conversation with her.

Laura had picked a bad time to come. His mother was downstairs, on one of the few occasions when she checked over the stock and dusted off rockers, spinning wheels, and antiquated hundred-year-old clocks. When Reggie introduced Laura to her, he saw his mother's lips purse, saw her eyes travel the full distance of Laura's young and —suddenly in the light of his mother's scrutiny—too ripe body.

Miss Ella said, "Are you interested in antiques?"

It sounded as though she meant, "Are *you* interested in antiques?"

"Oh, no," said Laura Lee, "I don't know beans about them. I came to see Reggie."

Miss Ella's face turned visibly pale. She turned abruptly and went upstairs.

"Did I say something wrong?"

"Mother doesn't feel well," Reggie said.

They had their first date that night. It was the only time Reginald Whittier had ever gone anywhere without telling his mother where he was going.

When he returned, the apartment was dark. She had not waited up for him. Momentarily, he believed he had been absolutely silly to imagine that his mother would have raised any objections to his going for a drive with Laura Lee, but when he tiptoed across to the bathroom, beside her bedroom, he heard her voice.

The words were loud and clear, said slowly and emphatically. "They go to and fro in the evening. They grin like a dog and run through the city!"

It was something from Psalms.

It was Miss Ella's way of telling him what she thought about the matter. She had done it before, whenever she disapproved of anything Reggie did, and he knew that if he were to mention it the following day, she would claim she had been sound asleep. She would say: "Maybe I was talking in my sleep. Folks *do*!"

That afternoon in May, at precisely the point when Brock Brown was talking to his headache, and Charles Berrey's father was suggesting that they all try to talk in words of one syllable, Miss Ella, in the apartment above Whittier's Wheel, was putting a worn, seventy-eight-speed record on the phonograph.

Below, her son was asking Laura Lee again: "Then it's all right? You'll be there waiting at ten-thirty in front of the college?"

"If you're sure you can get out," she said.

"I will, don't worry."

Suddenly, the militant sounds of "Onward Christian Soldiers" came from above.

"Oh, oh!" Reggie said.

"I don't see why she has to call you that way," said Laura.

"Mother doesn't like to shout at me, that's all. It's easier this way."

"Why can't she pick something else as a signal, some other song?"

But both knew it was a question for which no answer

was necessary. Miss Ella's ways were her ways. Reggie Whittier waited until Laura was outside and passing by the window. He gave her a two-fingered salute of so long, and she winked back. Then he went upstairs to see what his mother wanted this time.

PART TWO

Chapter Four

BROCK BROWN

Everything could have gone nicely that evening between Brock Brown and his stepmother if only Clara had not made that remark while she was draining the asparagus. Brock had looked forward to spending the evening with her. For one thing, when his father had to take the night shift at the garage, Clara never nagged at Brock. She never asked him why he didn't call up some friends, or go off to Murray's or drive by and see Carrie Bates. Clara hated to be alone.

For another thing, Brock wanted to make it up to Clara for using her money when he stole the green Mercury that afternoon. He wanted to be nice to her, laugh at her asinine jokes and pretend that he thought she was a very interesting person. He felt he owed it to her, just as he felt he owed it to the owner of the Mercury to leave money to make up for any inconvenience he had caused. That way, it was more like renting the car. Brock always left money behind whenever he took anything that was not his, and he never kept what he took, whether it was a car (which it usually was) or a lawn mower (once) or a string of outside Christmas tree lights (last winter).

Brock supposed Dr. Mannerheim could explain why he took things he did not really want. On the other hand, how serious *was* it? It wasn't very serious at all, Brock believed. There was no need to run to some head-shrinker for advice. He would grow out of it before long, and meanwhile, he was still a better person than most guys his own age—guys like Derby Wylie, who didn't care how he looked and did dirty things to girls all the time.

Clara's remark irritated him more than anything else because it simply wasn't true. That was one reason he had not said any more than "Oh?" in answer. Just oh.

She was standing there by the sink with a strainer in one hand, and the pot of asparagus in the other, and suddenly out of the blue she said: "When your father and I have a baby, we'll get a girl in to help."

"Oh?"

"I've never minded cooking. It's fun to cook. But housework gets me down."

"Sure."

"Well, it does. You try it some time."

"I believe you, Clara. You don't have to draw a diagram."

"What's got into you all of a sudden?"

"Nothing, for Pete's sake."

"I'm not complaining or anything, if that's what you think."

"I never said you were. Did I say you were?"

"Boy, talk about jigsaw puzzles. I'd like to put you together someday."

"Just forget about it, will you, Clara?"

"I would if I knew what I was forgetting about. You just flare up all of a sudden, Brock. No reason. No warning."

"Oh, for Pete's sake!"

"I'm telling you for your own good. You're a nice kid, but you flare up. I mean, no woman likes housework. Am I supposed to pretend I like housework?"

Brock did not bother to answer. All through dinner he brooded. Not at the fact Clara thought his father was going to let her have a baby. It would be a waste of time to even consider that. Instead, Brock thought about his car and the possibility that his father had not remembered to put the tarpaulin on the front seat. It wasn't easy to get grease off slip covers, even when you paid to have it done. There was also the possibility that some of the grease might rub off on Brock's clothes. Even if his father had remembered to put the tarpaulin there, what if he lent the car to one of the other mechanics at the garage, and *they* forgot; or just didn't know enough to leave the tarpaulin there? Plenty of times one of the mechanics had to go out on a call, and they didn't all have cars of their own. He should have let his father take the bus.

The argument did not start until long after dinner, a little past ten o'clock. In the meantime, Brock had spent most of his time polishing his shoes and straightening up his room, but toward ten he felt sorry for Clara. She was alone in the living room, watching television. Brock got a coke from the refrigerator and went in to join her. She was watching another quiz show—Cash-Answer this time. An eight-year-old boy had just named all forty-one signers of the Mayflower Compact. Drums were beating and bells were ringing and the quizmaster was screaming out: "You get cash for your answer, because it is correct!"

"He's probably a midget," said Brock, slumping down on the couch beside Clara.

"He's a genius. Eight years old and he's won $47,000!"

"He's probably some kind of nut," said Brock.

"I'd like to see *you* win that much money."

"So would I. But then, he's younger than I am. I'm jaded."

"Shh, Brock, listen. Jackie Paul's talking to him."

"Well, Charles—is that the name your friends call you —Charles?"

"Chuck, sir. I mean, Chuck."

"No reason to sir me, Chuck. You're the one with $47,-000!"

"Yes. I mean, I know it."

"Well, Chuck, how does it feel to be a celebrity? I bet you had an exciting day today."

"Yes, sir, Mr. Paul . . . Very exciting. We had dinner with my father's boss, head of Sterling Sporting Goods."

"There's a nice free plug if I ever heard one. You'll be a good businessman, Chuck."

"No, sir, I mean, Mr. Paul. I'm going to be a baseball player."

"A baseball player, huh?"

"Yes. Probably."

"I'm sure that if you make up your mind to be a baseball player, that's what you'll be, Chuck. I'm not worried about you! Not a bit! What else happened today?"

"My father said we should all talk in words of one syllable."

"Well now, that is a good joke. Words of one syllable, huh? I didn't know you even knew any one syllable words."

"Yes. And, and I have a cutlery—a knife collection."

"A knife collection. Boy oh boy! Whoops—there goes the signal. Time is up, Chuck! Until next week! See you next week, Chuck, and meanwhile, folks, remember if you suffer from nagging backaches . . ."

"Isn't that something!" said Clara. "A kid like that!"

"It's his memory, that's all."

"With all he knows, he wants to be a baseball player!"

"Maybe he wants to knife someone too," said Brock.

"Well, he's a real boy. He's not just a little bookworm. That's something!"

"What does he need knives for?"

"Lots of kids collect knives."

"I don't know of any."

"Oh, sure! Come on, Brock! Lots of boys collect knives. Just like snakes or anything else."

"If they do, they shouldn't," said Brock.

"Why shouldn't they?"

"They could hurt somebody, for Pete's sake, Clara!"

"Oh, pssssss!"

"They could! Somebody could get hurt."

"Brock, honestly!"

"A person could bleed to death."

"Who would bleed to death? Somebody could apply a tourniquet."

"A tourniquet! How many people know how to tie a tourniquet!"

It was one of those absurd, pointless arguments that sometimes happen between people, one that starts off in a random, picayune fashion, and then catapults to complete confusion, no longer random but wild and angry.

Clara said, "My father knew how to tie a tourniquet!"

"Almost nobody knows the first thing about tourniquets!"

"It has to be an awfully big wound anyway," said Clara, "for anyone to bleed to death."

"It *does not!* One knick of the old jugular and wham-o! Curtains!"

"Who's going to knife anyone in the head?"

"The head! The jugular is the trunk vein of the neck, in

case you ever get on Cash-Answer and they ask you, Clara!"

"You're plenty brilliant in your own living room, Brock, but you're not so great in the classroom, are you!"

"The jugular in the *head,* for Pete's sake!"

"That's not so crazy, Mr. Know-Everything! You're the one who's crazy, if you think people bleed to death in this day and age!"

Brock Brown stumbled to his feet, knocking the bottle of coke off the coffee table. "Don't you call me crazy!"

"Now, look what you've done. Made a mess!"

"You like messes, don't you? And dirt and grease? Come off it, Clara! You *like* dirt and grease!"

"*I* won't mop it up!"

"Leave it!"

Clara Brown looked over her shoulder at the window. She said, "Here comes your father!"

"If you think I'm so crazy, Clara, ask dad if people don't bleed to death."

"Calm down, now. Your father's had a hard day."

"Ask him," said Brock Brown, "because he can tell you! My mother bled to death, for your information!"

"That was childbirth. Now, calm down."

"Child *death,* you mean."

"All right, Brock. Okay, dear."

"And don't dear *me,*" said Brock Brown. "I'm not the one you want babies with!"

That evening in May when Robert Brown returned home, his mind was on getting away from Sykes over the Memorial Day weekend. It wasn't just because of what had happened earlier in the day. By now, he and Clara should know that any form of spontaneous love-making was a decided risk, with Brock in and out of the house all day. But it had been too long since the two of them had been alone together, somewhere away from Sykes. It would be good for both of them. It would even be good for Brock to be on his own for a couple of days. It wouldn't be very expensive, if they were to go somewhere near, like the Adirondacks, and maybe had a little more time to themselves and a more relaxed pattern of life, Clara might even get pregnant.

For himself, Robert Brown was not particularly anxious to have another child, but it would mean a great deal to

Clara. He supposed every woman (with the possible exception of Edith Brock) had a natural desire to be a mother. In a few years Brock would be going off to college, and it might even be fun to have a youngster in the house again. He was coming up the walk of his house that evening, thinking that he hoped it would be a girl this time—just to even things out—and thinking that the Adirondacks would be a perfect place for a vacation. He was totally unprepared for the collision with his son. Brock was running, and the pair collided head-on.

"Here, here!" Robert Brown laughed. "What's the rush?"

But his son did not laugh, nor did he smile or stop to talk. He shouted: "I just hope you didn't get the seat covers dirty!"

"I put the tarpaulin down," his father said smiling. "Besides I'm not hot out of the sewers or anything."

He thought of saying something more. Something less pleasant—perhaps: *"Where are you going at this hour?"* or *"Now, just wait a damn minute!"* but he could tell Brock was in one of his fits of temper. It happened now and then—not often, really, and it always blew over. Brock was a good kid. Sometimes Robert Brown even worried that Brock was too good, and that was a fool way for any father to feel about his son. No, Brock was one kid Robert Brown could be proud of. If a bad temper was the only flaw a boy had, a man might as well count his blessings. Robert Brown did—daily.

The first thing he saw when he entered the house was Clara on her hands and knees, wiping up something that had spilled on the floor.

He leaned down and kissed her forehead.

"What's up?" he said.

"Brock knocked over some coke."

"Well, why isn't Brock mopping it up?"

"Oh, you know him, Bob. Flew off the handle."

"There's no reason for you to clean up after him, honey."

"I don't mind."

"Did you two have a quarrel or something?"

"Not much of a quarrel," she smiled. "How was your day?"

The argument with Brock had upset Clara, but even in the few moments between his storming out of the house

and Robert Brown's entrance, she had been able to forgive Brock. It was her own fault, she believed, and she
had figured the whole thing out in the two minutes it
had taken her to walk to the kitchen, get a rag, and walk
back. The trouble was, she decided, that she had praised
that quiz kid on the television. Brock had an inferiority
complex, Clara reasoned, and it hadn't helped when she
had said that the eight-year-old was a genius. Added to
that, she had brought up Brock's marks at school. Sometimes Clara Brown could bite off her tongue. She knew
all about the way Brock's mother had neglected him when
he was a child—Robert had gone into that time and time
again with her—and she still couldn't think before she
spoke around the boy.

She supposed, too, that she had started him off earlier
in the kitchen, when she had said that she didn't like
housework. That probably made him feel this big! It probably made him feel as though she was tired of cleaning up
after him, and that in itself was preposterous, because
there wasn't a cleaner, more orderly boy than Robert
Brown's son.

Actually, Clara was disgusted with herself. It made her
feel a little better that she had lent Brock the ten dollars
that day. She just hoped he'd remember that, once he
cooled down, and she also hoped—much more—that Brock
would not repeat to his father the things she had said
that evening. Clara could not bear to disappoint Robert
Brown. Most of all she wanted him to keep on thinking
that she was a good wife, and that she would be an even
better mother.

"Are you sure Brock wasn't too hot-headed?" said Robert Brown, "because sometimes I wonder if he doesn't
need a little discipline."

"Don't be silly," said Clara.

And they both laughed then. Brock might need love,
and he might need reassurance; he might even need an
occasional ten dollars slipped to him on the sly, but where
could you find a better kid?

Brock Brown sat outside his house in the back seat of
the Chevy. He held the flashlight limply in his hand. He
had gone over the whole car, searching for grease marks
or stains, but there were none. He knew he would not stay
there long, only as long as he could. It wasn't fair that it

was happening to him again, twice in the same day. It could be easy to stop it, this slow pain beginning in his head, even easier than it had been that afternoon. At night, there were more cars parked in the streets, and there was less chance that anyone would see him take one. Yet he knew there was no easy out this time. His Junior Operator's license was not good after six o'clock. He knew plenty of guys his own age who drove after dark anyway, but Brock wasn't that kind.

He blinked the flashlight on and off, sighing and wiggling his toes in his shoes. He was motherless. Christ, Clara was no mother! Even if she did have a baby, she wasn't any mother, wouldn't be; but the hell with even thinking about it! She was going to have a baby just like the jugular vein was in the head! He laughed, and it made his head hurt more. He let the flashlight drop to the floor of the car and roll, and he thought: I don't have to pick it up immediately, let it roll around down there, but he retrieved it instantly, and put it in the side pocket where it belonged.

He had loved his mother. He had really *revered* her—that was the word. She understood him, for Christ's sake! What if his father had had his way and named Brock—the name he wanted—Robert Brown, Jr.? He would have been called Bob Brown, like a little nothing. Like John Smith or Tom Davis, or any other nothing name. He might even have been called Junior! Junior Brown . . . He remembered the way his mother used to tell his father: "I had to give up the name Brock to marry you, Robert!"

He could remember a lot of things about his mother, but why should he? She was dead . . . Filthy, she used to say, filthy. Or had he imagined that? What did she used to say? *You're a Brock.* Why did he remember filthy? He thought of his father's hands. There was always dirt under the nails, dirt that never seemed to go away, no matter how his dad scrubbed. That wasn't his dad's fault. He was a mechanic.

Now it was worse. Brock could feel the pain in his head begin to get in line. The bandeau. He got out of the car, moving slowly so as not to jar his head too much. He began walking, going down the street by the tar-line in the center. He remembered the way he had swung out of the school parking lot that afternoon, with Dr. Mannerheim looking at him, and Carrie Bates. Why hadn't he thought to turn the radio to some station playing classical music? Why did he always think of things too late? Maybe he wouldn't have even been able to find any classical music on the radio if he *had* thought of it. Nobody had a chance anymore. It was all rock 'n' roll. And he wasn't that kind of guy. *"You're a Brock."*

The Rubins' house on the corner was dark. Jews were nice people; goddam Hitler! Brock had read in a book once that the Nazis tied women's legs together when they were having babies. Oh, Christ! Oh, Christ! What kind of a lousy world was it?

Brock went up the gravel driveway of the Rubins' house. He could hear the crunch of his shoes on the gravel under him. Maybe someone else would hear the noise—Mr. or Mrs. Rubin—and they'd call out *Who's there?* If they did, he wouldn't run. He wasn't a sneak. He'd just stand there and take it. More than any Nazi'd do.

The lawn was wet with night dew. There was a birdbath midway between the garage and the back porch. It was nice of the Rubins to care about birds. They were really swell people, and Brock was glad they lived on Marvin Avenue. His headache had reached the tip of his ear now, in a full arc. He was on the first step of the back porch, and with his right hand he reached out to try the screen door. It was locked.

He began to perspire. Why had they locked it? Why in hell? What was so valuable on the goddam porch? By the light of the streetlamp on the corner, he could see a few things on the porch. A mop, a stepladder, some plants, and a pail. Why had they locked the screen door, for Christ's sake? The door beyond, the wooden one leading into the house, was shut. That was probably locked too, Brock could understand that. But why the screen door? He didn't want to break in. He wasn't a housebreaker! But what choice did he have now?

He was in a cold sweat. He could get pneumonia, for Pete's sake. He had run out without even taking a coat. His head was splitting, right down the middle in two even halves. From his trousers he took out his jackknife. He went up another step and held on to the iron door handle with one hand while he tried to cut the screen with the other. He could only make a hole. After he forced the hole more, so that it was wider, he stuck his finger in and flipped the catch. The screen door was open.

Before he went in, he felt in his pockets for change. He had seventy-two cents. Was that enough? He decided it was more than enough. The screen door squeaked as he held it open, reaching over for one of the plants. He held the plant under his arm and dropped the money on the ledge. His headache was at its peak now. Carefully, he let the screen door shut and began walking across the lawn with the plant. It wasn't until Brock was halfway down the gravel drive that he realized water was leaking out of the bottom of the pot—dirty water, leaking down on his pants. He dropped the plant instantly! Even his hands were dirty. The plant and the pot spilled to the ground, and Brock kicked them angrily. What a rotten trick! What a rotten thing to happen! Dirty Jews! Dirty Jews! And he began to run, with tears stinging his eyes.

His headache was gone, but in its place was a sudden wave of nausea. He ducked into the shrubbery, two doors from his house. He knelt and retched. He looked down at his hands. They were as dirty as the wet earth he was kneeling in. From some time far gone, he heard a voice saying: "You're a little pig! You and your father belong in a sty!"

He began to sob. "I can't help it! I can't help it!"

"Filthy little pig!"

In a small boy's voice, Brock Brown began to pray: "Make her die, God! Kill her! Make her die!"

But his prayers had been answered some nine years ago.

Chapter Five

REGINALD WHITTIER

Above Whittier's Wheel, in Miss Ella's living room that May evening shortly after ten o'clock, the trio sat facing the television set. Miss Ella rocked back and forth in her chair, and Reggie Whittier sat beside Mr. Danker on the worn mauve couch with the claw legs. It was the second time this week that Mr. Danker had been invited to dinner. After Laura Lee left the antique shop that afternoon and Reggie went upstairs to see what his mother wanted, Miss

Ella had said to him in a coy, saccharin tone: "There's a surprise tonight, Reginald."

"What would that be, mother?"

"Mr. Danker's coming over."

"He was just here Sunday."

"Why, Reginald! I'm surprised at you, Mr. Danker thinks the world and all of you."

"I didn't mean anything."

"You're like a son to him. Why, we're practically his family."

"I like Mr. Danker, mother."

"Then why aren't you pleased?"

"I'm not displeased."

"You don't have any other plans, do you, Reginald?"

"I may go out later."

"Now, don't be a silly boy! Where would you go at that hour of night? Mr. Danker will stay to watch Cash-Answer. It'll be midnight before he leaves."

"Mother," Reginald Whittier said, "would Mr. Danker mind so much if I were to go out for awhile?"

"You want to watch Cash-Answer, don't you, Reginald? I bought the set for you."

"I know that, mother."

"Then let's not talk silly," said Miss Ella.

His mother had cooked Reggie's favorite food. Chicken and mashed potatoes and fresh peas. Mr. Danker brought along a copy of the *National Geographic Magazine*. There was an article in it about the scenic playgrounds and historic shrines of the United States and Canada. Mr. Danker wanted to show Reggie the pictures of the Haleakala Crater in Hawaii National Park, where he had visited as a boy.

"Not much older than you are," Mr. Danker had said, squeezing Reggie's knee as they sat beside one another on the couch. "Someday maybe Miss Ella will let you go there with me, for a little vacation."

"Reginald will be twenty soon," said Miss Ella from the kitchen, "and when he's twenty, it just might be a good idea. I've always thought travel was wasted on the young. But twenty's nearly a man!"

"Wouldn't you like that, Reggie?" Mr. Danker asked. "A nice vacation off in Hawaii?"

"Sure," said the boy.

"We could swim, and fish, and get you a nice tan, eh Reggie?"

"Sure, Mr. Danker."

Miss Ella said, "Reginald has very sensitive skin. It doesn't take to the sun."

"I've been in the sun plenty of times, mother."

"Oh, I know that, Reginald. But you know yourself you always turn that awful red color that makes you look odd. Some people look fine after sun exposure, but you don't, Reginald. You're fair-skinned."

Mr. Danker said, "Never mind. You've got those nice baby-blue eyes, Reggie. That's all you need."

"Doesn't he have nice eyes, Mr. Danker?"

"Very nice eyes," Mr. Danker answered. "I wish I had such nice eyes."

Reggie sighed. "What else about Hawaii?" he asked.

Miss Ella said, "His eyes are the color of a summer sky!"

"They certainly are!" said Mr. Danker.

"Everyone has something nice about them," said Reggie's mother. "Everyone has one good point. Reggie's eyes are his good point. It makes up for his stuttering. God is fair."

"Reggie has nice hands too," said Mr. Danker.

Reggie wished they would stop talking about him. He bit his lip and sighed a second time.

His mother said, "When he was a little boy, I used to kiss his hands and tell him God made them for him to do good deeds with."

"That's right," said Mr. Danker. "You're a lucky boy, Reggie, to have your mother love you the way she does. My mother, God rest her soul, was the same kind of woman. When she passed, I felt as though part of me went with her. Part of me just died with her."

"Just how big is that Haleakala Crater?" Reggie asked.

"Well," said Mr. Danker, stretching out his arms so that his right arm passed across Reggie's shoulder, "It's huge. It's bigger than the whole island of Manhattan." He let his right hand drop on Reggie's shoulder and rest there. "It's big, all right!"

Miss Ella said, "Dinner will be served in two minutes. Are you boys comfortable in there?"

"We certainly are," said Mr. Danker, pressing his hand against Reggie's back.

Now dinner was over. They had watched Mystery Hour and the Happy Honey Family. Now they were watching Cash-Answer. Reggie glanced at his watch in a nervous, surreptitious gesture. The quizmaster's voice blared in the room: "*All right, Chuck. For forty-seven thou-sand doll-ars, name the forty-one signers of the Mayflower Compact!*"

On the screen there was a close-up of the eight-year-old's face as he puzzled over the question, while the music played in the time allotted for him to think out his answer.

Mr. Danker sat forward on the couch, counting on his fingers.

"Let's see. There was William Mullins, Edward Tilly, William White, Edward Doty, John Tilly, Francis Cooke —let see, Myles Standish, of course—Gilbert Winslow—"

"*Time is up,*" the quizmaster's voice shouted.

". . . Issac Allerton," said Mr. Danker, "John Goodman, William White—"

"You said William White," said Miss Ella.

"I did?"

"Yes, you said William White. Now, shhhh! Listen!"

"Samuel Fuller," said Mr. Danker, "Degory Prist, Steph——"

Reginald Whittier's mother said, "Shhhh! Mr. Danker! Listen!"

It was ten past ten by Reggie's wristwatch. He was supposed to meet Laura Lee at ten-thirty in front of the college. He sat wondering how he would get out of there; could he just stand up and walk out?

The quizmaster was screaming: "*You get cash for your answer, because your answer is correct!*"

Mr. Danker said, "I knew them all."

"You named William White twice," said Miss Ella.

"But I knew them. It was a very simple question."

"I'd never force a boy of mine to that extent," said Miss Ella. "As far as I'm concerned, a boy should be the best of whatever he is." She smiled across at Reginald. "If you can't be a pine on the top of the hill, Be a scrub in the valley—but be, The best little scrub by the side of the rill; Be a bush if you can't be a tree!"

It made Reggie think of the Lees' trailer; of the way he had hit his head on the bunk bed when he had bent over to get in it with Laura. He remembered how he had thought: *You've got to do it someday, Reggie, if you ever want to grow up and be a man.* He remembered how he had thought: *Be a pine, Reggie! Don't let her keep you a scrub!*

Mr. Danker said, "I know the second verse to that poem!"

In unison, Miss Ella and Mr. Danker recited:

"We can't all be captains, we've got to be crew,
There's something for all of us here;
There's big work to do, and there's lesser to do,
And the task we must do is the near."

Miss Ella laughed. "That was fun!"

"I know that poem," said Mr. Danker.

"I like to think of it as my touchstone," said Reggie's mother.

"It's got some good sound advice in it," Mr. Danker said.

Reggie stood up. The *National Geographic Magazine* fell from his lap to the floor. Miss Ella looked at him with surprise.

"What's the matter, Reginald?"

"I have to go somewhere, mother."

"Go *where?*"

"Somewhere," Reggie said. "I have an appointment."

"At twenty minutes after ten in the evening?"

"Why, even Stoker's is closed," Mr. Danker said. "The last show is just letting out down at the Green Mountain Theater."

"I'm not going to a drugstore, and I'm not going to a movie," said Reggie. "I'm going to meet a girl!"

"I don't know what kind of a girl would be willing to meet a boy at this hour," said Miss Ella, "do you, Mr. Danker?"

"I daresay I don't," Mr. Danker answered.

"Don't pretend," said Reggie, "just don't sit and pretend!"

"You're starting to stutter, Reginald."

"I never stopped stuttering, mother!"

"You're embarrassing me before Mr. Danker, Reginald."

"This is no way to behave to your mother," Mr. Danker said.

"I'm going out. That's all. I'm going out."

"Go ahead," said Miss Ella. "Go right on along. No one

will stand in your way, Reginald. Go right on along."

"Mother, is there anything *wrong* with my seeing a girl?"

"That depends on the girl," said Mr. Danker.

"There's nothing wrong with the girl!" Reggie shouted.

"Don't try to reason with him, Mr. Danker. He'll not listen to reason. He'll find a way to put us both to shame."

"I'm going," said Reggie. "And there's nothing wrong with it."

He walked to the hallway and grabbed his jacket. "I'll be back later."

"Don't bring any diseases into *this* house," his mother said.

Mr. Danker said, "Reggie—wait!"

But Reginald Whittier slammed the door. He went down the back stairs to the street. The car was parked in front of Whittier's Wheel, and Reggie climbed in. Then he remembered. He had left the keys behind in his room. He would have to go back for the keys.

Suddenly, Miles Danker was standing beside the car.

He said, "I brought your keys, Reggie."

"Thanks."

Reggie held his hand out.

"I'll give them to you in a few minutes. I want to talk to you first."

"I'm late, Mr. Danker."

"That kind of girl will wait," said Mr. Danker. "Just don't worry about that."

Mr. Danker walked around to the other side of the car and got in. He sat sideways, facing Reggie. Reggie looked straight ahead.

"What do you know about women?" Mr. Danker said.

"You ought to know. You made the speech about them, Mr. Danker, a long time ago."

"Three years ago, Reggie. Only three years ago. You're still a boy."

"I'm not a boy, Mr. Danker. I'm a grown man." Reggie said, "Why can't I be treated like one?"

"Do you want to go for a drive and talk, Reggie?"

"Yes. But with the girl who's waiting for me, Mr. Danker."

"A girl like that," Mr. Danker said, "What do you know about a girl like that. A maid!"

"I knew you and mother knew where I was going. Why do you pretend?"

"Because we both know more about this kind of girl than you do, Reggie."

"You're not even married, Mr. Danker."

"Do you think I'd bring a whore to my mother's house? Do you think I'd violate my mother's memory that way?"

"Mr. Danker, I'm not going to meet a whore, and I'm not going to bring her to my mother's house."

"She was in the shop today, wasn't she, Reggie?"

"You know everything, don't you? All the signers of the Mayflower Compact, and who was in and out of the shop today."

"Why do you want to hurt me, Reggie? Because you hurt me everytime you're sarcastic."

"I wasn't sarcastic before now, Mr. Danker. I'm sorry if I am sarcastic, but I want to keep my appointment."

Mr. Danker said, "You were sarcastic earlier, Reggie. Earlier, when I was telling Miss Ella and you how dear my mother was to me. The minute I finished saying that, Reggie, you asked me how big the Haleakala Crater was. Now, if that isn't sarcasm, what is it? It was your tone of voice. You were snide, Reggie. Snide. I tried to ignore it, but for heaven's sake, Reggie, I'm human. I have feelings!"

"I'm sorry, Mr. Danker."

"I know you don't mean to hurt me, Reggie."

"No, I don't want to hurt you. I like you, Mr. Danker, but I'm late as it is."

"Do you know what that girl will want you to do, Reggie?"

"Nothing," said Reggie, "Nothing!"

"All right, Reggie, I'm afraid I'm going to have to be brutal. I hoped I wouldn't have to be brutal, but I'm going to have to be!"

Reggie turned his head and looked at Miles Danker. He was reaching into his coat pocket for something.

"What are you doing, for the love of Pete, Mr. Danker?"

"Turn on the dashboard lights, Reggie. I want you to see something."

"What?"

"Turn on the dashboard lights, Reginald."

Reggie leaned across and flipped the switch. Mr. Danker passed him a packet of cards.

"What is it?" said Reggie.

"Look at them carefully, Reggie," said Mr. Danker, "I hate to be brutal, but Miss Ella's asked me to be a father to you. It isn't easy for a boy to grow up without a man to guide him, and I want to guide you, Reggie. Guide you along the right path."

"Oh, jeez! Jeez!"

Mounted on the cards were pictures of men and women —pornographic pictures, one after the other.

"Look at every single one of them, Reggie," said Mr. Danker.

"Where'd you get these?"

"You think because I'm not married, I don't know about women, Reggie? You look at those pictures. How do they make you feel, Reggie?"

Reginald Whittier lied. "I don't feel anything. They're dirty pictures, that's all."

"Is that what this girl wants from you, Reggie? This *maid?*"

"No, Mr. Danker," Reggie said.

"Then why are you stuttering?"

Reggie dropped the cards on the car seat. "Give me the keys, Mr. Danker."

"Do you want to go for a drive, Reggie? We'll talk."

"I want to keep my appointment."

"You *still* do?"

"Mr. Danker, please take your cards and give me my keys."

Miles Danker reached for the cards, his hand brushing Reginald Whittier's trousers. Reggie jumped.

"What's the trouble, Reggie?"

"Will you give me my keys, please?"

"Your mother wouldn't mind if we went for a drive. She'd like that a whole lot better than your meeting that maid."

"The keys, Mr. Danker!"

Reggie held out his palm, and Miles Danker placed the keys there, his fingers touching Reggie's skin. A pang of revulsion shot through Reggie. He shoved the keys in and turned over the motor.

Mr. Danker smiled. "All right," he said, "all right,

Reggie. But we'll go for a drive another time. Don't think I don't know you by now. You won't have any fun with that girl!"

"What does that mean?" said Reggie.

"Oh, *you* know." Mr. Danker opened the car door and got out. He said, "I won't say 'have a good time,' because you won't have a good time. Wait and see, Reggie. We're a lot alike, you know. A lot alike!"

For the first time since he had ever thought of the possibility that Laura Lee might really be pregnant, Reginald Whittier, backing away from Whittier's Wheel with Mr. Danker's paunchy figure framed in the headlights, just hoped to God she was.

Chapter Six

CHARLES BERREY

The Berrey family were on their way back to Reddton, New Jersey. Charles Berrey was curled up in the back seat of the car, pretending to be asleep, while his father and mother sat in front arguing. The car was passing through the Holland Tunnel, and the argument was so intense that neither bothered to turn down the radio. Charles made a face at the sound of the static, and buried his head in his arms.

Evelyn Berrey was saying, "Well, I simply won't stand for it! We're not going to lie to *Life* magazine!"

"They probably won't even print it."

"What do you mean they won't print it? You know they'll print it! 'Quiz kid gets a B in English!' I can see it now!"

"I didn't tell Chuck to say that to the *Life* reporters. I told him to say it to Mr. Carter. We were going to spoof Mr. Carter, that's all. It was his own idea to tell *Life*."

"A 'B' in English. English is Chuckles' best subject!"

"Evelyn, it was Chuck's own idea to say that to *Life*. Think of the kid, for God's sake, instead of yourself all the time! Do you think he wants to be known as some kind of oddball genius?"

"He *is* a genius!"

"He is *not* a genius! He has a good memory, and that's that!"

"I think you're jealous of him, Howard Berrey."

"That's a laugh!"

"I think you'd have liked it if *Life* had interviewed *you* instead of Chuckles."

"I've had my picture in the paper plenty of times. Pull-enty of times!"

"Oh, sure! And I'm Princess Margaret."

"Back at Mizzou it was Duke Berrey this and Duke Berrey that. Why, my mug was plastered all over the place!" Howard Berrey chuckled. "I used to get tired of seeing it."

"Poor thing."

"I actually did. After a while I even stopped clipping out the pieces on me. I remember mom got mad because I stopped sending them home. She said, 'What do I have to do, take out a subscription to the Missouri papers myself?' " He laughed. "I told her, 'What's the matter, you don't know what I look like by now?' " He took his right hand off the wheel, holding his thumb and his first finger wide apart. "She had a scrapbook this thick on me."

"I'll just bet there wasn't any mention of your *grades.*"

"Evelyn, what college did *you* go to, hmm?"

"I'm not pretending to be anything but what I am," said his wife. "And I'm not forcing my son to lie about his school marks!"

"I never forced Chuck to do anything. I've never laid a hand on either of my kids, and you know damn well!"

"Knife collection! Baseball player when he grows up! Where'd he get that stuff?"

"Turn the radio off, for God's sake! You always have the radio on, or the television going. How many times have I walked into empty rooms and found the radio on or the television going?"

"He hates his knife collection," said Evelyn Berrey, pushing the radio's "off" button as they drove out of the tunnel. "There's one thing you can't do, Howard—you can't make a sow's ear out of a silk purse!"

"Very witty, aren't you, Evelyn? Very witty! I'm surprised *Life* didn't interview *you.*"

"I hope Paul Carter gives you a bonus for that free plug Chuckles gave Sterling."

"What have you got against Mr. Carter, Evelyn?"

"It would take all night."

"I respect Paul Carter."

"Oh, don't I *know* it!"

"He was very impressed with Chuck."

"You should have made Chuckles tell him he *flunked* English! Maybe he'd have been all the more impressed!"

"You should have had all girls, Evelyn. You never understood Howie, and you don't understand Chuck."

"*I* don't understand Howie?"

"You told me yourself—you just couldn't figure out why Howie married that Italian."

"I suppose *you* understand it, though."

"You bet I do!"

"Would I be prying if I asked exactly why?"

"Because they're good in bed, that's why."

"You don't care what you say in front of your son, do you?"

"He's asleep, Evelyn. Even geniuses need sleep."

Charles Berrey sat curled up in the corner of the back seat with his eyes shut. He wondered how his father knew that Howie's wife was good in bed. At the same time, he was amazed to know that girls were bad in bed too. He had never thought of that before, and it posed an interesting problem. If girls did it too, *how* did they do it? Girls didn't have anything to do it with, did they? Charles was sure of that. Maybe Italian girls did. Yet his father said that Italian girls were *good* in bed. Maybe all girls but Italian girls were made differently. None of it was logical. . . . Charles Berrey was bad in bed sometimes too . . . Often. In fact, if his father ever found out about him, it would be a catastrophe. He decided then and there never to do it again. There would have to be an oath on it, to make it real.

Charles Berrey often took oaths. Yesterday he had taken an oath on his mother's eyesight that he would not set fire again to the grass around the trash can in the backyard. One of his weekly duties was to carry the trash out and burn it. Charles liked that duty. Fire was magic. Charles had read many myths about the origin of fire. His favorite was a Polynesian myth. There was a boy named Maui, whose grandmother was the goddess of fire. Maui asked her to make some fire, and when she did, she made so much that it came out of her fingers and her toes, and everything around her began to burn. The rain came finally and put the fire out, but there was still some left in the trees. According to the Polynesian myth, the fire left in the trees was the source for all of mankind.

When Charles burned the trash out behind his house, he liked to pretend about this myth. He took his squirt-gun with him, and after he set fire to the trash can, he touched a match to the grass around it. After the grass had burned a little while, he squirted water at it and put the fire out, but in the trash can, fire still raged. It was a game with him, but his mother said a grass fire could get out of control, and if he didn't stop the game, she would never allow him to touch matches again. He knew the only way to make himself stop was to take an oath, which he had—yesterday afternoon. Now he would never do it again, or his mother would go blind.

Charles decided his new oath—the one about not being bad in bed anymore—would be an oath on his father's life. He wished there were some way to tell his father his decision, to let his father know how much he wanted to please him, but there wasn't any way to do it.

Charles Berrey wished too that his mother and father would stop quarreling. The trouble was, they were both right. His mother was right about Charles not liking his knife collection and not wanting to be a baseball player when he grew up. At the same time, his father was right about having had his picture in the newspapers when he was in college, and about Mr. Carter. Charles had liked Mr. Carter very much. And Mr. Carter had paid for every-one's dinner in the restaurant.

When Mr. Carter said, "I just wish I could get *my* boy's nose in a book!" Charles had beamed and looked at his father's face to see his expression. It had surprised him that his father was not smiling, but frowning instead.

His father said: "Don't get the wrong idea. Chuck's not *all* books, you know!"

That was when Charles and his father spoofed Mr. Car-ter—told him about the "B" in English.

"Is *that* right!" said Mr. Carter.

"Yes, sir," said Charles. He giggled, and then he no-ticed that his father smiled at last. Charles felt proud to be collaborating with him.

His mother said nothing, but her eyes were cold and angry.

"Well, now, nobody's perfect," said Mr. Carter, "A boy

that got perfect grades and knew the answers to everything just wouldn't be normal."

"Last week," Charles said, "When I had to name all the kings of Israel and Judah, I barely remembered Uzziah."

That was an untruth. Charles Berrey would never forget Uzziah's name. Uzziah had come down with leprosy for burning incense in the temple. Would Charles ever forget the picture in his mind of Uzziah standing with the burning taper, while the leprosy popped out on his forehead? What was it Charles' mother always said? *Play with fire and you get burned, one way or the other.*

"I didn't know you almost forgot Uzziah, Chuck!" said his father, grinning down happily at him.

"What do you think I am, a brain or something?" Charles answered.

Everyone had a good laugh over that, everyone but Charles Berrey's mother.

In June, when he took his tests, Charles decided, he would purposely answer some of the questions wrong. He sat in the booth of the restaurant poking at his ice cream with his spoon, no longer interested in dessert, thinking only that in June he would spoof them all! For some reason, his decision made him feel tired and no longer glad. He sighed and sat there, watching the chocolate melt on the spoon and dribble down into the dish. An infinitesimal part of Charles Berrey was protesting the way a dog who had been spanked for another dog's mischef might protest, by cowering there in the corner, uncertain and sad, with something akin to anger stiffled deep inside of him—so deep that it would probably never be born at all.

Evelyn and Howard Berrey argued all the way from the Holland Tunnel to Reddton. Charles feigned sleep so well that when they reached the bungalow on Almanac Drive, his foot was actually asleep from staying in one position so long. He shook it and squeezed his toes inside his shoes, and when he got out of the back seat, he stumbled into his father.

"I beg your pardon," he said.

"Just say you're *sorry*, Chuck!" his father snapped.

"Yes, sir."

"Leave him alone, Howard! You make me sick!" said his mother, slamming the car door.

"Oh, shut your yap, Evelyn!"

"I'll shut mine when you shut yours!"

"You're asking for it, Evelyn! You've been asking for it all night!"

"You make me sick! Come on, Chuckles," said his mother, putting her arm around the boy's shoulder.

"That's right, come to mommy, Chuckles," said Howard Berrey in an angry, mock falsetto.

Charles tried to laugh at the way his father imitated his mother, but he was a little afraid now. He had only seen his father strike her once, but he knew that it had happened other times too. Sometimes during the night he woke up and heard his mother crying: "Don't hit me, Howard!" and invariably after she said that, there would be a crash, and Charles' room would seem to vibrate with the noise of it.

The one time he had actually seen it happen, he had never forgotten. They had all gone on a picnic near Palisades. Charles was coming back from a walk by himself, with a butterfly caught in his hand. It was a zebra swallowtail, the kind with the largest tail of any native species. He was sure it was a zebra, even though he knew they were more common to the Southeast. He was running to show them, the excitement mounting as he drew near the spot in the woods where they were preparing lunch. Just as he came to a point where he had a glimpse of them, standing there in the clearing, he opened his mouth to shout: "Look what I found!" but he never got the words out. His father had reached out and hit his mother across the face with the palm of his hand. The blow had sent her sprawling to the ground. Charles stood dead still, staring. The first thing he saw was his mother's face—the expression there. It was peculiar, all squeezed up. He had never seen her cry before, and it took him a moment to realize that was what she was doing—crying. When he looked down at the rest of her, he saw her skirt up above her knees, saw the flaccid white flesh of her thigh, and there against the white, a trickle of red blood, and her gartar holding her stocking. He turned and darted back behind the tree where they couldn't see him, and he stood there for a moment with his heart pounding wildly under his sweater. After some slow seconds, he realized that the inevitable had happened. He had wet his pants. He stood there with his fists clenched, hating himself, afraid of what his father would do to him when he found out, and a few slow seconds later, when he looked down at his hand, he saw that he had killed the zebra swallowtail.

Charles never told them about the zebra, nor about what he had seen. He sneaked away from there and scampered down the rocks to the water, and then he sat in the water. Later, he told his mother he had slipped and fell into it, and that was why he was all wet. When his mother began to scold him for it, his father said: "Let the boy alone. All boys do that!"

Inside the house, that night at the end of May, Charles and his mother had milk and cookies in the kitchen, while his father put the car in the garage.

"You're sleepy, aren't you, Chuckles?" said Mrs. Berrey.

"Please don't call me Chuckles."

"I've always called you Chuckles, darling. Don't you like me to have a special name for my big boy?"

"It's a preposterous name."

"Oh, it *is*, is it?" his mother laughed. "Do you want to 'iterate that?"

"*Reiterate*," said Charles Berrey giggling.

"Maybe I'll call you Mr. Iterate instead."

Charles laughed so hard he almost choked on his milk.

"That's what I'll call you, Mr. Iterate."

"I'll call you Mrs. Amphigoric then!"

"Mrs. *what?*"

"That means meaningless."

"Figorick! Where do you pick up those words, hmmm?" She pinched his cheek. "Did you swallow the dictionary?"

"I masticated it," said Charles.

Mrs. Berrey's smile faded. "What did you say?" she said.

"I masticated it."

"All right, that's enough play for tonight," his mother said somewhat coolly. "That's enough for tonight."

"What's the matter?" he said.

"Go to bed, Chuckles. Hurry now!"

"I will," he said, finishing his milk, puzzled at her sudden change of mood.

Instead of hugging him hard, the way she usually did when they said goodnight, she simply bent and kissed his forehead.

"Go right to sleep, Chuckles," she told him.

For awhile, after he was undressed and in his pajamas, Charles Berrey thumbed through Ironside's *British Painting Since 1939*, but he was not as fascinated with it now as he had been late that afternoon. He kept trying to figure out why his mother had acted as though she were angry with him when they were in the kitchen, toward the end. He would never have dared to show off his vocabulary around his father, but his mother usually enjoyed it. Maybe he had gone too far when he had called her Mrs. Amphigoric. Tomorrow he would remember to explain to her that the word amphigoric came from the word amphigory, and all amphigory meant was a nonsense verse. He shouldn't have told her it meant meaningless. He had probably hurt her feelings.

When he put out the light above his bed, he lay in the dark thinking about what his father had said earlier. He was glad he had made up his mind to be good in bed, like Howie's wife, but it still confused him. Why were only Italian women good in bed? It might have something to do with the fact that they were all Catholics, and Catholics were extremely religious. Religious people would not be bad in bed. Maybe what his father had meant to say, was that *Catholic* women were always good in bed. He was pondering over this when the argument started in the living room. This one was even worse than the one on the trip home. In the car, Charles had not worried as much, because his father could not very well become violent in traffic, but now there was nothing to stop him.

Charles crawled out of bed and listened at the door. He did not have to open the door to hear what they were saying because the bungalow walls were paper-thin, and both of them were yelling.

". . . never teach him any respect!" his mother was screeching, "No wonder he's mixed up!"

"He's not mixed up, you're mixed up! Your brains are scrambled, Evelyn, scrambled and fried!"

"If he's going to lie to *Life* magazine, who's he going to lie to next?"

"What the hell do I care about *Life* magazine!" said his father, "I don't even read *Life* magazine!"

"You mean you don't even *read!*"

"Shut your yap!"

"He never said anything like that before tonight. That's

all I know. Not before tonight, he didn't. You're the one that put it into his head to be a smart aleck."

Charles Berrey stood anxiously by his door, wondering if he shouldn't go in there and tell her what amphigoric meant right now, instead of waiting until tomorrow. She had taken it all wrong.

"You're the one that told him to lie about his grades," said his mother. "Now he's going to be a smart aleck."

"What's wrong with that? I'd rather have him be a smart aleck than a goddam book-sissy!"

"You'd rather have him stand right there in *that* kitchen and tell his own mother he masturbated the dictionary?"

"He was making a joke!"

"A smutty, smark-aleck, wise-guy joke! In front of his own mother, in that kitchen, *right here tonight!*"

"I'm glad he knows the word. I was beginning to wonder if there was something wrong with him, reading in the goddam library all day and night!"

"What kind of a father are you? You want your own son to masturbate!"

"What's he supposed to do?" said his father, "go out and screw eight-year-olds in the recess yard? Berrey men always grow up fast!"

Charles Berrey sank onto the edge of his bed. His face was red-hot with shame. He bit on his knuckles and jiggled his knees. That wasn't what he had said at all; he had *never* said that word! Not even to himself! Everything was crazy suddenly. There was his father in there saying he didn't care if he was bad in bed, and only tonight he said Howie had married Jean because she was good. His mother had mixed everything up, and his father didn't even know it, and Charles didn't know anymore who was right and who was wrong. The shouting was growing louder and louder now, and Charles was frightened and sick of listening. He didn't know why he got up and went across to his closet in the dark, nor why he reached for his wool jacket on the hook behind the door.

"Shut your yap!" he heard his father say, "or I'll give it to you good, Evelyn!"

"Go ahead and hit me!" his mother shouted back. "Just you go ahead and hit me!"

When he heard the crash, he ran to the window.

The night was cool and not too dark because of the moon. It hadn't been much of a drop to the ground. The only hard part was getting the screen unhooked without anyone hearing the noise when it fell off onto the sidewalk below. But even that was easy, because the Berrey bungalow was wild with the sounds of his mother and father screaming and throwing things. Were they just throwing things, or had his father hit her? Charles Berrey read the newspapers every single day, and they were full of stories about men murdering their wives, and women murdering their husbands. Sometimes even children murdered their mothers and fathers. If he could stop them some way, or make someone stop them. If he could find a policeman, or do something.

For awhile he simply stood out behind the garage by the trash can. There were matches in his coat pocket left over from burning the trash yesterday, and he thought of the dry grass, half-burnt already, and of the oath he had taken on his mother's eyesight not to set fire to it anymore. He thought of Uzziah coming down with leprosy in the temple while he was burning the incense; and he thought of the rain pouring down in the Polynesian myth, and Maui's grandmother with fire coming out of her fingers and toes.

From inside the house, he heard another crash, and now he began to run, back through the fields behind his house, running and crying and wetting his pajama pants. His bedslippers were thin-soled and he could feel every bump and stone, but he ran as fast as he could, without knowing where he was going or how he was going to get help. When his feet hit pavement, he realized he was on Rider Avenue, and when he stopped, breathless and wet and desperate, he saw the red firebox on the corner. He didn't even bother to use the little iron mallet to break the glass, but with his whole strength, punched it with his fist until it smashed. Then, with his other hand, he pulled down the handle.

It would only be a matter of minutes now. Charles Berrey knew that. Soon the fire engines would roar and clang, and lights would go on in all the dark houses, and people in robes would lean out of their windows, and everyone would wonder where the fire was.

70 THE TWISTED ONES

It was near midnight. In Sykes, New York, a boy named Brock Brown was secretly retrieving seventy-two cents he had left on a neighbor's screen porch; and in Auburn, Vermont, Reginald Whittier was asking Laura Lee to elope with him. Charles Berrey climbed back in the window of the bungalow and waited.

PART THREE

PART THREE

Chapter Seven

BROCK BROWN

The Memorial Day weekend was three days away.

Clara Brown wanted to be sure that nothing would interfere with the trip to the Adirondacks which she and Robert had planned. She knew that her husband was worried about Brock, about what had happened two nights ago. He sat across from her at the table, frowning, only picking at the stew she had prepared for their lunch.

She said, "Bob?"

"Hmmm?"

"Are you thinking about Brock again?"

"I'm sorry, Clara."

"Bob, it's the first time he's ever gotten into any trouble," she said. "Besides, he really *didn't* get into trouble. It's all straightened out now. It was just a misunderstanding."

Clara Brown didn't really believe that. Whatever Brock had been doing on the Rubins' back porch when Mr. Rubin caught him, Clara Brown did not believe Brock's story that he was only trying to warn the Rubins that someone was stealing their plants. Mr. Rubin had found him trying the door that led into the Rubins' house. Brock said a man—a big, bushy-haired man—had run down their driveway carrying a plant, and that Brock had startled him in the dark, and that then he had gone to warn the Rubins.

Estelle Rubin had been very nice about it. She had

73

thanked Brock, and told Robert Brown that she was sorry there had been some confusion about the matter; and she had said that she had found her poor petunia all smashed in the driveway. But Sam Rubin had acted doubtful and suspicious. Why would a big, bushy-haired man want to steal a petunia plant, *he* wanted to know, and if what Brock said was true, why hadn't Brock just rung the Rubins' doorbell?

Brock said he was too upset to think straight.

"What were you doing down by the Rubins' at midnight anyway?" Robert Brown had asked.

And Brock had answered. "I was just taking a walk. Clara and I had had a little quarrel, and I was just simmering down. Just walking around. You saw me when I left the house, dad."

Robert Brown said, "That was about ten-forty-five. What were you doing for an hour and a quarter?"

"I told you, dad. Just walking around."

Maybe he really *was* telling the truth. Clara didn't know. But Brock's story certainly sounded fishy.

Robert Brown put his fork down at the lunch table and sighed. "I *hope* it was simply a misunderstanding," he said.

"Of course it was, Bob. Brock wouldn't have any reason to be snooping around the Rubins' house."

"I wouldn't think so."

"What would he want to snoop around the Rubins' house for?"

"I don't know, Clara. But why were his clothes so dirty? That's what I don't understand. You know how Brock is about keeping everything clean. The knees of his pants were dirty, remember?"

"He explained that. He said he knelt down to see what the bushy-haired man had dropped."

"The plant was dropped on the driveway, Clara. That's a gravel driveway."

"I don't think we should dwell on the matter, as though Brock was a criminal or something, Bob."

"Bushy-haired stranger!" said Robert Brown. "It sounds phony. Like that murder case a few years back, when that fellow killed his wife."

"That's what I mean," said Clara. "They didn't believe he was innocent either. There was a bushy-haired man in that case, and no one believed it."

"Did you?"

"Of course! Of course I did! All through the trial, I could just feel it in my bones."

"Well, I wish I could feel it in *my* bones about Brock."

"Bob, you know something. You're just spoiled, that's what."

"Spoiled?"

"That's right. Brock's such a good boy, you're just not used to having the slightest little thing go wrong where he's concerned."

"Clara, the Rubins are our neighbors. I do all Sam Rubins' work for him. Only last Monday, I sold him a new set of tires."

"Sam'll get over it."

"I *hope* so."

"Estelle was as nice as pie to me today. She waved and smiled when I got off the bus, and she was as nice as pie."

"I just wish I knew if Brock was telling the truth. I'd be sore as hell at Sam Rubin for thinking Brock was up to something, if I could just believe Brock."

"I believe him."

"And you believe a bushy-haired man took one of the Rubins' plants."

"There are plenty of nuts loose, Bob. They're not all locked up in the loony-bin."

"He'd have to be a nut to cut through somebody's screen just to steal a plant."

"You read about nuts in the newspapers every day, Bob. Every day you read about another nut."

"I suppose so, Clara. I suppose so."

"It'll do us both good to get away for awhile. Do you suppose it'll be warm enough for shorts in the mountains?"

"Probably not."

"That's good, because I don't have any that fit anymore. Since last summer, I've gained about ten pounds. Imagine?"

"Clara?"

"What?"

"Do you honestly think Brock will be okay while we're gone?"

"I'm not worried one single bit about Brock," said Clara Brown that May noon, "not one single bit."

And that much was true. Whatever the truth was about

the other night, the wife of Robert Brown saw nothing
even remotely ominous in Brock's recent behavior. In
Clara's mind, the very worst explanation she could come
up with, for Brock's being on the Rubins' back porch, was
that Brock might have been trying to see in their windows. There were two windows on the porch, and Brock
could very well have been looking in them. Estelle Rubin
was always running around in her backyard wearing
practically nothing at all, and she might very well have
aroused Brock's curiosity. After all, he was a shy, bashful
boy . . . What did Brock know about women?

Clara thought it might even be possible that Brock *had*
cut the hole in the screen so he could go and look in the
windows, and that he might have heard Mr. Rubin coming and thrown the plant out on the driveway and in-
vented that story. Put dirt on his clothes and made up
that story about the big, bushy-haired man, so that the
Rubins wouldn't know he'd been spying on them.

That was the very worst Clara could imagine, and it
seemed to her that even *that* was not really very serious.
Brock had never done anything wrong before, and if the
worst was true, he never would again. She had never seen
Brock as frightened as he was that night, with Sam
Rubin scowling at him, and Brock quaking, with his face
drained of color. In the long run, Clara supposed, it was
a good thing. It had taught Brock a lesson.

"I suppose it would be silly to postpone our trip," said
Robert Brown, picking up his fork, "I guess I am spoiled.
Brock's a good kid."

Robert Brown, at high noon that day in late May, was
at last reconvinced of this. Brock's story about the bushy-
haired stranger could very well be absolutely true. Only a
few days ago, the garage had gotten a call to pick up a
green Mercury on a back country road. It had been stolen,
it turned out, and the thief had tied a ten-dollar bill to
the steering wheel with a rubber band. Then just abandoned it, in the middle of nowhere. Clara was right.
There were a lot of nuts around, even right here in Sykes,
New York.

At Sykes High, the class in general psych had seven
minutes to go. Brock Brown had not heard a word Dr.
Mannerheim had said. His mind was striped with
thoughts of the night at the Rubins', and Carrie Bates. Car-

rie sat across from him, and she was coming on again.
She had been "on" the whole hour, staring directly at him,
turned sideways in her seat, so that it was obvious to
Brock and everyone else in the class. Some of the guys
were snickering and glancing back in Brock's direction,
and the girls were busy scribbling notes furiously to each
other. At the very beginning of the hour, Brock had found
a note on his desk. It said:

"You look like Montgomery Clift ... C. B."

He had not bothered to answer her note, nor even to
look in her direction. It had angered him that he had
been unable to keep the flush of color from spreading
across his face to his ears, as he read the note; and he was
furious with himself for grinning the way he had to. He
hadn't wanted to smile. It happened without his being
able to control it—the same way it happened when anyone told him someone they knew had died, or someone
they knew was very sick. He'd just stand smiling, without
being able to do anything about it. The other night, he
had even smiled when Mr. Rubin caught ahold of his
shirt collar and said: "What the hell are you doing?"

"Nothing," Brock had answered, trying to shrug his
shoulders, with that silly grin on his face. His knees were
shaking under his trousers, and his stomach had flipped
over with fear, but he just said, "Nothing," and grinned
at Sam Rubin.

"You were trying to break in here, weren't you?"

"No, Mr. Rubin. I was trying to warn you."

He had had no time to think up a better lie. Everything
had happened suddenly. Brock was not sure why he had
tried the Rubins' door on the screen porch, but he was
afraid about it. He remembered only that he had decided
to go back there and get his seventy-two cents, which he
had left on the ledge for taking the plant. After all, he
really hadn't taken the plant. It was there in the driveway. When he left the bushes, where he had gotten sick
to his stomach, he had wanted his money back. That part
didn't make him afraid. He was entitled to his money; it
was his own money.

But what had happened next worried him. Next he
had seen the knob of the door that led into the Rubins'
house. He had put his hand on it, let his fingers curl
around it and feel the brass, and he had thought: *I have
to go in there. . . .* What had he wanted to do? That was

what he couldn't figure out, or remember anymore. It had something to do with the fact his clothes were soiled. That wasn't his fault. He hadn't made himself dirty. The plant was responsible for that—the hole in the bottom of the flowerpot, and the dirty water that leaked out of it. But why did he want to go inside the Rubins' house? To *get* them for it? Had he thought something about getting them for it? That was the creepy part. That was what shook him up. And he *was* all shook up; boy cat, all shook up.

Brock had his sunglasses on in the classroom. He had decided to leave them on all day. They looked good. He was wearing dark brown against tan today, and the frames of his sunglasses added to the over-all effect. They were shell frames, brown ones. Before he had left the house that morning, Clara had asked: "Who are you being today, Brock?"

"What does that mean exactly, Clara?"

"Movie star, international spy, who?"

"I'm that quiz kid on Cash-Answer," he had told her. "I just won 44,000 dollars for knowing the jugular vein is the trunk vein in the neck."

"Congratulations," Clara had said.

"It was nothing at all."

"Anyway, Brock, you look very handsome. You're a very handsome boy. Did anyone ever tell you that?"

"*You* did, if *you're* anyone."

"Come on, Brock, let's patch things up."

"You mean, before Memorial Day, Clara? So you can go away with a clear conscience?"

"I'm not the one with a guilty conscience."

"You don't have *any* conscience."

"What is it, Brock? What's gotten into you the last few days?"

"I guess I just hate housework," Brock had said. "I guess I'll just be glad when you and dad have a baby, and a girl comes in to do the housework."

"Don't try to be funny, Brock. I told you I didn't mean that about hating housework."

"Maybe I really *am* crazy, Clara. Maybe I'll get so crazy I'll just burst and bleed to death, unless someone comes along and applies a tourniquet."

"Will you ever forget *anything?*"

"No, I have a very good memory. Just like that little quiz kid."

"Well, you better remember to stay away from people's back porches while your father and I are away in the mountains," Clara had said.

Brock had thought about that while he drove to school that morning. He hadn't had a headache since the night at Rubins', but what if he got one over Memorial Day weekend? What then? It would be okay. His father would leave him extra money. He said he was going to leave him some money; and what if he *did* get a headache? There were worse things than taking somebody's car for a ride, or taking somebody's goddam flowerpot! He'd never take a flowerpot again. Everything would have been all right, if he hadn't picked out that goddam flowerpot. It couldn't happen to him again in a million thousand years . . . Could it?

Brock knew plenty of guys that wouldn't even give a second thought to what had happened at the Rubins'. Compared to other guys, Brock was a crazy angel, about as shook up as Clara, and she was a lump of clay. Other guys were running around in their dirty cars doing things to girls. Pawing them and mauling them. More than that, too. Brock had seen the inside of Derby Wylie's old Ford, and it was knee-deep in rubbish. Old newspapers and magazines, and buttons pinned all over everywhere saying sexy things like: "I want yours!" and "Give it to me, baby!" . . . Brock sighed. Sure, Brock knew about other guys. Rock 'n' roll and run around the way they did, and Carrie Bates went right along with them. Brock wasn't that kind of guy.

"What the hell are you doing?" Mr. Rubin had wanted to know.

And all he could do was answer, "Nothing." Grinning like that.

He wished he could stop thinking about it. Something else bothered him. When his father had said, "What were you doing for an hour and a quarter?" Brock had wondered about that himself. Was there something he couldn't remember? The part in the bushes, when he had got sick to his stomach, was fuzzy. He thought he might have been crying, but that was too crazy. He wouldn't cry. Had he gone somewhere, or had he done something he didn't recall?

While he was sitting there in psych thinking this, another note landed on his desk. Carrie Bates had passed it to the boy in front of him, and the boy had reached back and dropped it by Brock's inkwell. This time, Brock wasn't even going to read it. He might not be perfect—he knew he wasn't—but he wasn't like the other guys, he wasn't that bad. Carrie Bates could come on all she wanted. She could turn herself inside out. Brock wasn't going to have anything to do with any girl! No one could ever accuse him of that!

He took the note and stuffed it into his pants pocket. His hand brushed against the key he had there. All right, he had a key! Was he a criminal because he had taken a key! He didn't even know where the key fit, did he? He only knew that while his father and Clara and Mr. and Mrs. Rubin were all arguing in the Rubins' living room that night, he had seen the key on the hall table. He had put it in his pocket. That was all. Maybe it didn't even belong to the Rubins. Maybe someone had left it there. He wasn't sure it was a key that would fit any of the Rubins' locks . . . But why had he taken it? Why did he want it? What was he keeping it for?

I, Brock Brown, boy cat and all shook up, have this key—

No, that wasn't what he meant. What he meant was that he was afraid. The Memorial Day weekend was only three days away, and he was afraid. He really needed a head-shrinker this time. Now he really needed one. So for the second time during that hour, Brock Brown decided that he would wait after class, wait and talk to Dr. Mannerheim. Just for a second. Just for a half a second.

Dr. Clyde Mannerheim, that noon in late May, was starving. He was always hungry this last hour before lunch, but this morning he had overslept and missed breakfast. A cup of coffee had had to suffice, and the last minutes of the hour were dragging now, seemingly interminable.

Mannerheim was not a real doctor, not an M.D. He was a Ph.D. He had majored in art history at Princeton, and after he had gotten his M.A. in the same subject, his interest had focused on psychology. For one thing, there were very few positions of any real challenge in the art history field. He could do museum work, or gallery work, or teach, but none of those prospects made him enthusiastic. Psychology did. Mannerheim had wanted to become a clinical psychologist, or perhaps even a psychologist with a private practice, an analytic psychologist. He had finished up his Ph.D. in art history, and then turned to courses in psychology. When the money ran out, he had only eighteen hours of psychology behind him. He could have found a better position teaching art history, but Clyde Mannerheim had dreams of going on with his studies in psychology, of taking summers off to pursue this dream, and he had accepted the offer from Sykes High as a temporary stopover on the way.

◄Teen-agers were fascinating creatures—full of inhibitions, guilty over everything that was natural to life, and unashamed of everything that was unnatural. What was that weird, unnatural dance they all performed so expertly? The fish. Gyrating and undulating as though that were their whole purpose on this earth; yet gasping and turning red if ever he mentioned a word like "intercourse" in his discussions. He did not even have to mean *sexual* intercourse. The word intercourse alone was enough to set them off. Bernard Shaw had been right—youth was wasted on the young. They went through their teens drugged by their super-egos, doped up on wicked fairy tales their parents passed on to them about the male and the female; poisoned by the examples their mothers and fathers presented to them—some of them never recovering from it, but forever doomed to the mediocre idea that sex was a sinful act, permissible only under the dullest circumstances of an equally dull marriage. Those who did recover from it often found that by the time they did they were middle-aged; there was a divorce or two behind them, and unpaid analyst bills.

It was just a wonder to Clyde Mannerheim that the young ever survived their youth.

When the bell finally rang that hour, Mannerheim gave a sigh of relief as the students whipped out the door. He was fishing in his desk drawer for his bag of sandwiches, prior to going to the teachers' lounge to brew coffee and eat his lunch in peace. His wife was pregnant again, and he had decided to cut down on the cafeteria expenses, so every day he brought his lunch. His hand was just touching the brown paper bag in the bottom drawer when a voice spoke.

"Dr. Mannerheim?"

He looked up and saw Brock Brown standing by his desk.

Brown puzzled him somewhat. He seemed always on the verge of wanting to tell him something, but was never able to get the words out. Once or twice before, Brown had brought books to him, asking him to explain something in the books. Invariably they were very advanced psychological studies, too advanced for Brown, Mannerheim had decided long ago. They were Brown's excuse for talking with him. He knew that, but he could never bring Brown to speak his mind.

Clyde Mannerheim also knew that there was something going on between Carrie Bates and the Brown boy. He had noticed that often in the last morning hour. The Bates girl did everything to get Brock Brown's attention, while Brown did everything to pretend he was not interested. Mannerheim suspected that Brown and this girl had had some dealings outside school. This was no bashful girl—bashful boy relationship. For one thing, Carrie Bates was not the least bit shy. For another, whatever was on the Brown boy's mind, Carrie Bates had something to do with it. Clyde Mannerheim had watched the pair for some time now, and he was sure of it.

Teen-agers, Mannerheim thought, poor stumbling creatures. He remembered his own teens, and how he had very nearly tried to commit suicide, because he felt so intensely guilty over the fact he had not controlled himself one night with a girl he had been seeing for two years. The next day she had put an end to their relationship—even though she had not tried to stop him the night before— and Mannerheim had gone to the river near his house and stared into it, thinking that he was the vilest, most foul, most sinful young man in existence.

"What can I do for you, Brock?" said Mannerheim.

"I don't want to keep you, sir. You're going to lunch, aren't you?"

"I'm not all that hungry," Mannerheim answered, smiling. "What's on your mind?"

The boy laughed, passing his hand through his short-cropped black hair. "I guess I'm all shook up," he said.

"You and Elvis, eh?"

"I don't like rock 'n' roll. Don't get me wrong."

"No? I was noticing your sideburns," said Mannerheim

smiling again. "Brock, there's nothing wrong with rock
'n' roll. Do you think there is?"

"It's not good music."

"But you don't have to feel guilty because you like it."

"I don't like it, Dr. Mannerheim. And I don't like Elvis
Presley. These sideburns aren't like his."

"Maybe not, Brock."

"I just think when a man wears his hair cut real short
on the top, it looks good to have it inch down a little by
the ears."

"It *does* look good."

"But I'm not shook up that way," said the boy. "You
know what shook up means? It's just a word. It doesn't
mean someone goes running around all over the place
acting like other guys."

"What are you shook up *about,* Brock?"

"Nothing, really. I didn't do anything wrong. Not
really."

"Can you tell me a little more, Brock?"

"If you want to go eat lunch, go right ahead, Dr. Mannerheim. You know, I'm not desperate."

"I don't want to eat lunch, Brock."

"The whole thing's crazy anyway. I wouldn't know how
to say it, even if I did have time."

"You have plenty of time."

"Sure," said the boy, "right through to Memorial
Day." He laughed and shoved his hands in his pocket.

"Go on, Brock."

"You hear all the time about guys running around
with girls, Dr. Mannerheim. I mean . . ." he stopped what
he was saying, and shuffled his feet. "That isn't what I
mean. I guess I don't know how to say it. Put it this way.
My name is Brock. My first name. It was my mother's
maiden name, Dr. Mannerheim. She died. I felt bad
about that. You know, what boy wants his mother to die?
What kind of a boy would want his mother to die?" He
paused again. "That isn't what I mean. I don't know
what that's got to do with what I mean. I don't know
what murder's got to do with it."

"Murder, Brock?"

"Death. My mother died. She was giving birth."

Clyde Mannerheim thought a moment. Then he said,
"Lots of times youngsters wish their parents dead. It's a

very normal thing. But if one of their parents die, then sometimes they feel responsible, because they wished for it. Of course, they aren't responsible at all."

"Do you think I wished my mother dead?"

"Did you, Brock?"

"I revered her. I do revere her. Her memory. I'm not that kind. I don't even know what we're talking about anymore."

"You started by saying something about your first name."

"That's right. Brock. It was my mother's maiden name."

"And?"

"Well, it's a different name. I guess I'm different too, sort of. All shook up, or something. But I've never done anything really wrong, not like other guys."

"What have you done, Brock?"

"It's sort of perverse or something. Not abnormal. I don't mean abnormal. It's the most normal thing in the world, but—"

The boy was playing with a key now, tossing it from one hand to another.

"What's perverse about it?" said Clyde Mannerheim.

He remembered again the way he had felt, staring into the river that night, remembered how he had thought, Lord, God, what if mother ever finds this out. He supposed every boy felt some unconscious incest guilt about sexual relations with girls. Particularly if the girl was a "nice" girl. In Brock's case, it might be a much more guilt-ridden situation. His mother had died in childbirth. He probably felt, unconsciously, that he might kill a "nice" girl if he were to have relations with her, just as his father had killed his mother by getting her pregnant. Maybe Brock Brown was trying to tell him that he had done something with the Bates girl. Maybe that was why he tried so hard to ignore the Bates girl. He was afraid of what he had done.

"You see this key?" said Brock. "It fits some lock."

With his left hand, he pushed the key through a hole he made with the fingers of his right hand.

It was all too clear to Dr. Clyde Mannerheim.

He said, "Go on, Brock."

"You'll think I'm—I don't know what you'll think," said Brock Brown. "In fact, I don't even want to discuss it any more."

"We haven't discussed it *yet*."

"You better go eat your lunch, Dr. Mannerheim."

"I told you, Brock. I'm not hungry."

"Well, I am. I'm going to eat mine. Down in the cafeteria."

"Are you sure you want to leave now, Brock? You got this far."

"There's nothing to tell, really. I didn't do anything, really. I did something, but I'm not going to run around talking about it."

"It won't get any farther than me," said Dr. Mannerheim. "If it's about a girl, her name is safe with me."

"It's not about a girl! It's not about a girl!" Brock shouted.

Clyde Mannerheim realized his mistake. He should never have forced it that far. He said, "All right. Okay, Brock."

"What kind of a guy do you think I am anyway?" Brock said.

"A nice guy, Brock."

"What I was talking about—" he stopped in the middle of his sentence, and shoved the key back in the pocket of his trousers. "I'm going to have my lunch now, Dr. Mannerheim," he said, sighing.

To Mannerheim, the symbol of the key was obvious. Now that Brock had put it back in his pants, the matter was closed; there would be no more conversation on the subject. Yet Clyde Mannerheim could not let this boy walk out of his classroom feeling as though he were perverse, or evil, or sinful, simply because of an involvement with a girl. There had been no one to help Clyde Mannerheim some twenty-five years ago, but there was someone to help Brock Brown—even if it was only a moment's reassurance, even if it was just a masked reference to the subject, some slight clue he might offer the boy to help him out of the mire of guilt and self-recrimination.

"Wait a minute, Brock," said Clyde Mannerheim as the boy turned to go. "I want to tell you something."

"Yes?"

"Think about this, Brock. Think carefully about it. You mentioned perversion. Things that seem perverse."

"Yes."

"There's only one real perversion in this world, Brock. Just one. Do you know what that is?"

The boy shook his head.

"It's chastity," said Clyde Mannerheim. "Chastity."

The boy stood momentarily staring at him, his eyes fixed on Mannerheim with some thin veil of alarm to their expression. It would take awhile for him to realize the meaning of Mannerheim's words, but Clyde Mannerheim sat back in his swivel chair with the feeling of a job well done. "Think about it, Brock," he repeated.

Wordlessly, Brock Brown turned and went out the door.

Chapter Eight

REGINALD WHITTIER

At high noon that day in May, Reginald Whittier and Laura Lee were married by a justice of the peace, just outside the capital of Vermont, in a small town called White River Junction. When they returned to Montpelier, they bought a sack of hot dogs and some soda pop, and took it to their room. For two days, they had been staying in a tourist home.

Between them, they had twenty-six dollars and ten cents left. On the night they had eloped, they had the fifty dollars that Laura had just been paid and the four Reggie had in his wallet. They had no change of clothes, and neither had succeeded yet in getting a job. At night, Reggie slept on top of two pillows on the floor, while Laura occupied the double bed. The first night they had tried sleeping in the same bed, but Reggie just could not fall asleep. He wasn't used to it, he apologized. After he got work, they'd find a place with single beds. Laura understood perfectly, she said; things would work out.

Last night they had gone to a movie. It was a very mushy affair, about two newly-weds whose parents thought they were too young to marry. Reggie kept getting up to go out and have a cigarette during the love scenes. He had bought his first pack of cigarettes yesterday afternoon, and Laura had tried to teach him how to inhale, but he couldn't seem to get the knack of it.

"I suppose I shouldn't smoke at all," he told her after he tried for a while. "It gives you cancer anyway."

But when they had left the movie and were walking back to the tourist home, he said: "I guess I have the cigarette habit. I kept wanting one all through the picture."

"It wasn't a very good picture," said Laura.

"It wasn't the picture," said he. "I really wanted to smoke."

She said, "Reggie?"

"What?"

"Are you sure you don't want me to go to the doctor and find out for sure before we go through with it tomorrow?"

"I want to marry you," he answered. "Either way."

"Are you sure?"

"Things will be different when we're married."

She said, "I'm not complaining or anything."

"We decided to get married, didn't we?" he said, "You left your folks the note and everything."

"I wouldn't have to go back to Auburn, if we didn't get married. I could go to New York or someplace. I'd be all right."

"I want to marry you," he said.

In a way, Reggie Whittier did believe that things would be better after they were married; and in a way, he did want to marry her. He believed this, and he wanted this, because he could not bring himself to admit that the elopement had been the sudden, thoughtless, angry inspiration it was. He could not chalk this up as another failure, as more proof that he really was the scrub in the valley his mother always told him to be.

But since he had left Auburn, Vermont, left without a word or a note to his mother, he felt as though he were a stranger in a foreign country. Only once before in his lifetime had he experienced this feeling. That was the summer he attended the Boy Scout Jamboree in Edgewater, New York, against Miss Ella's wishes. It was the summer he was thirteen, the summer he joined the Scouts. The Scoutmaster, a young, sturdy fellow who managed Stoker's Drugs, had encouraged him to join, and then at meetings paid special attention to Reggie, giving him wild praise for his feeble attempts at tying diamond knots and figure-of-eights, awarding him this merit badge and that, with enthusiastic reassurance, and ultimately accomplishing the near-impossible by convincing Reggie to do something Miss Ella disapproved of.

The Scoutmaster did not go along on the Jamboree, however. Few of the boys who did go cared the least bit about knots or merit badges. Reggie was mosquito-bitten, tongue-tied and lonely at the end of twenty-four hours, and at the end of forty-eight, he came down with impetigo. Mr. Danker drove down from Auburn to get him, and when he arrived at Whittier's Wheel, Miss Ella ignored him for three days, until in a burst of nervous, remorseful tears, Reggie told her she had been right. He sobbed out the whole story—how there had been bugs in the Welsh rabbit, how the boys had short-sheeted his bed and called him Bugs Bunny because of his stutter, how the tent had leaked during the rain the first night, and how much he had missed her. Especially how much he had missed her.

His mother applied soothing ointment to his impetigo, saying, "We'll just forgive and forget, Reginald. We'll just forgive, and forget all about the Boy Scouts of America.

"Just remember," she said. "If you can't be a highway, then just be a trail."

Reggie Whittier sat on the double bed in the tourist home that noon, munching his hot dog while Laura made up her face. She was going to apply for a job as a waitress at the Montpelier Tavern.

"What I can't figure out," said Reggie, "is why mother hasn't done anything."

"Stop worrying about it, Reggie. All that's behind us."

"It's her car, you know. I mean, she gave it to me, but it's registered in her name. She could have called the police."

"I'm going to write my folks a long letter tonight. Dad's probably cooled off by now. You know, they eloped—mom and dad. In Sarasota. Jeez. Mom was only sixteen."

"What's that gluck?"

"This? Mascara."

"Oh."

"What's the matter with mascara? Everyone uses it. All the movie stars use it."

"I never saw anybody use it."

"Everyone uses it! Is there something wrong with it?"

"You sure use a lot of makeup, Laura."

"Don't you like it?"

"Sure. I like it. I just said you sure use a lot of it."

"It sounds like you don't like it."

"I do. I really like it."

"I'm not kidding, Reggie. All girls use it. Oh, I suppose your mother never did. But then, *she* never would."

"You don't have to say that."

"What are you so touchy about? You told me yourself you're glad to be on your own."

"It's just that you don't have to say things against her."

"I wasn't, Reg. I just said she wouldn't use mascara."

"You said, *she* wouldn't," he said. "It was the way you said it."

"All right, I'm sorry."

"She's not such a *bad* person, you know."

"Did I say she was?"

He wadded up the wax paper from the hot dog and tossed it into the wastebasket. "They'd certainly find us if they were looking for us," he said. "After all, we're right in the state capital."

"They *aren't* looking for us. You know what?" she said, "I bet we're both good riddance, as far as they're concerned."

"No. You don't know my mother."

"Maybe *you* don't know her. She hasn't tried to find you, has she?"

"Mother's funny about some things," he said. "She might be just sitting back and waiting."

"For what?"

"Well, she usually doesn't try to stop me from doing anything. She usually just lets me find out for myself that it was a bad idea."

"Thanks. Thanks a batch."

"I didn't mean it that way."

"It wasn't my idea, you know. I don't even think I *am* pregnant."

"I didn't mean it that way, Laura." He reached for a cigarette and struck a match. "I'm glad we're married."

"Some honeymoon."

"You knew, Laura—you knew how it'd be."

"If you're going to smoke," she said walking across to him, "at least try again to learn how to inhale. Here, give it to me." She drew in on the cigarette. "See?"

"I don't see that I'm doing very much different from what you're doing."

"You have to get it down into your lungs. Take a drag and breathe in, Reg."

"All right."

He took it from her hand and tried. This time he didn't cough or choke.

"Much better!" she said. "Much better, Reggie!"

"I'll try it again," he said, "I think I'm getting it."

She watched him while he sucked in on the cigarette a second time. "You got it, now! That's it! That's right!"

"I did it okay?"

"Honey, you inhaled! That's what you did! You inhaled!"

"I did?"

"Sure! How do you feel?"

"Not too dizzy."

"It makes you feel a little dizzy, but you'll get over that. That's great, Reggie. It took *me* weeks and weeks."

He sat on the double bed grinning up at her.

"See how easy it is?" she said.

"It *was* easy, Laur."

"I'm so proud of you, Reg!"

She bent over and put her arms around his neck. "I'm so proud of you!" she said. "Hey, what's the matter? Am I poison or something."

"It isn't that. I didn't mean to pull away."

"I'm your wife, remember, Reg?"

"I was afraid of the lipstick. You don't want to smear your lipstick."

"For you, I'll take it off," she said. She took a Kleenex from the pocket of her skirt and wiped her mouth. "There."

He sat there not moving.

"Well, how about a kiss, Reggie?"

"Sure," he said, getting up awkwardly. "I'll kiss you."

He started to lean forward, without putting his hands on her.

She said, "Reggie, listen. We're married now. I know we're not in love, but we're married. You have to get used to me."

"I want to," he said.

"It's like inhaling or anything else. It's easy, once you're used to it."

"I feel a lot for you, Laur."

"And you know something else, Reg? You're not stuttering as much when you say w's any more. Do you know that?"

He smiled. "I didn't even notice."

"Well, I noticed."

"Shall I kiss you now?"

"Would you?"

He walked up to her and put his arms around her. He brought his mouth down on hers in a hard, crushing movement. She pushed him back after a moment. "Go easy," she said. "Don't try to be a cave man. Just go easy with me."

She said, "Let me show you." Gently, she placed one hand on the back of his head, her fingers running up under his hair. The other hand, she put around his waist. Then she kissed him. He didn't move.

"You're not kissing me back," she said.

"I was so. I was standing here."

"But you weren't doing anything. You were just standing there!"

"You were showing me, weren't you?"

"You can't kiss somebody who doesn't want to be kissed."

"I want to be kissed!" he shouted. "I want to be kissed!"

Laura burst out laughing, holding her sides. "Oh, gosh, Reggie—oh, for the love of heaven—"

"Well, I do!" he said angrily. "What's the matter with you, anyway?"

"I'm not laughing at you."

"Then what's so funny?"

"I'm laughing at the old lady who runs this place. Can you imagine what she's thinking, rocking away downstairs, with you up here yelling: *I want to be kissed.*"

Reggie's mouth tipped in a half-hearted grin. "I suppose it does sound kind of funny."

"Sure, it does. Honeymooners, for the love of heaven!"

Reggie began to grin a little more. "Dopes. That's us!"

"We'll be all right, Reggie. You'll see."

"I know it. I'm not worried, Laur."

"I'm going to the doctor right after I try for the job. I'll find out for sure, Reggie." She reached out and poked his shoulder with her finger. "If we're going to have a baby, you'll have to learn how to kiss."

"I want to learn, Laur. I want to learn everything."

"You and me are going to have a lot of fun, Reggie. We might even fall in love."

"Wh-wh-we mi-mi-"

"We might!" she said emphatically, "and that's the first time I noticed your stuttering all day."

Chapter Nine

CHARLES BERREY

At noon in Reddton, New Jersey, Chuckles was home from school for lunch.

This day in May, lunch was not the gleeful, teasing affair it usually was. Evelyn Berrey set the soup before her son without a word, and Chuckles did not even glance up at her. He was busy reading a book on baseball, which his father had bought for him. The relationship between mother and son had taken a sharp turn for the worst. Ever since that night a few days back, when Howard Berrey had very nearly broken her ribs, Evelyn Berrey and Chuckles had only the very bleakest sort of communication.

The way Evelyn Berrey saw it, Howard had turned Chuckles against her. After she had been knocked to the floor of the living room by her husband, there had been a false alarm in the neighborhood. The fire trucks had roared to the corner of Rider Avenue and Jones Street, and Howard had left her sprawled there and run out to see what had happened.

Searching for some small degree of comfort, Evelyn Berrey had pulled herself to her feet and hobbled in to see Chuckles. He was standing by the window, fussing with the screen. His hand was cut and bleeding, and on the floor his coat lay—with more blood on it.

Her first thought was that someone had come through the window and tried to attack poor Chuckles, but when she saw the coat, she realized that it was Chuckles himself who had come through the window. Where had he been, she demanded, at such an hour? Just where had he been? Just what was he doing, climbing in and out of windows at midnight, running around all bloody?

She was unable to elicit a word from the boy, but when Howard Berrey returned to report that someone had turned in an alarm on Rider Avenue, everything was all too clear.

And so it began:

"I'm going to turn you into the police," said Evelyn Berrey.

"Do you want me to give it to you again, Evelyn?"

"Howard, are you completely out of your mind! He just turned in a false alarm!"

"Get out of here, Evelyn!"

"I won't! I will not! I'm going to call the police. What kind of a smart aleck trick is this, hah? Is this another one of your bright ideas, Howard?"

"Chuck, answer your mother's question. Was this *my* idea?"

"No," Chuckles said. "I did it myself."

"Why? What's the matter with you? Look at you, all blood! Howard, is this your idea of a son?"

"Okay! He turned in a false alarm! All right!"

"All right?"

"Chuck, go wash your hands and put iodine on."

"I'm going to tell the police, Howard!"

"Are you sappy or something? How the hell do you think it would look? 'Quiz kid turns in false alarm.' Put that in your goddam *Life* magazine!"

"You drove him to this!"

"Shut your yap! Kids turn in false alarms plenty of times."

"Oh, I see. I didn't understand that. Now that I understand that, I'll just go off to bed and get a good night's sleep. Thanks for helping me understand that, Howard."

"Chuck, I told you to go wash your hands!"

"Maybe he wants to turn in another alarm before morning, Howard. I mean, kids turn in two or three alarms a night, don't they?"

"Go turn yourself in, Evelyn."

"I'm going to! To a hospital! And just find out how many of my ribs are broken!"

"They're all broken, Evelyn. That's why you're able to stand there and yell at me so well."

"From here on in, he's your worry, Howard. You're captain, from here on in."

"It's about time!"

"Just send him out to turn in false alarms and break windows and run through the streets at midnight, Howard. Like all kids."

"Will you ever shut up?"

"Yes, right now. I'm through! He's your worry. He can say what he wants to, do what he wants to—anything he feels like!"

"Get out of here. I'll talk to him when he comes back."

"That's right, Howard! You take care of everything, dear. You just take care of everything, and Chuckles will *end up in hell!*"

Evelyn Berrey had stormed out of the room and gone to bed. For three days since then, it had been the same. Chuckles barely spoke to her, and she spoke to him only when it was absolutely necessary. It was father and son now, teamed up against her. There was this "confab" and that "confab," and Chuckles was catching ball out in the backyard with Howard nights after Howard got home, telling Howard ball scores from a hundred years back and completely ignoring Evelyn Berrey. Well, let him, she decided. Let Chuckles just wait and see how much his *father* understood him. He'd find out soon enough which side his bread was buttered on, and meanwhile, Evelyn Berrey could wait!

From the kitchen, she shouted in to him, "You eat every bit of that, Chuckles. And don't read while you're eating!"

No answer. Well, just give him time.

"And change your Band-Aid," she added. "It's filthy!"

Still no answer. His hand would get infected, and *then* he'd see who knew best! Howard never payed any attention to things like that. To Howard, iodine was the answer to everything. Put a little iodine on it, he always said, and then he forgot. Dirt, germs, stones—nothing could hurt if there was a little iodine on it. That was Howard for you. Get the bandage as filthy rotten as you liked! There was iodine on it, wasn't there? That was Howard all over the place!

Evelyn Berrey said a little more gently, "Chuckles, I mean that about changing the Band-Aid. You'll do that, won't you?"

"Yes," he said.

Just yes, ah? Well, Howard could pat himself on the back

this time. This time he'd done a rip-snorting job. Chuckles was treating her like she was a hired hand. Congratulations, Howard, Evelyn Berrey thought, and many happy returns of the day. Just don't come crawling to me when anything goes wrong around the place. This is your little castle now, Howard. Your castle. Your son, your everything. Take it and like it!

Charles Berrey sipped the pea soup wondering just how long it would take his mother to come to her senses. Didn't she know that he had done it for her? She might be dead if he hadn't done it. He read in the newspapers everyday about men murdering their wives, and she had already been knocked down when the fire engines arrived. It had happened in the knick of time. Didn't she know that?

Now she was angry with him because of it. She had wanted to tell the police on him. If she was going to turn against him, *he* could show her. He would be on his father's side. It wasn't easy to be on his father's side, because he was never quite sure what was expected of him, but he was *on* his side anyway. He remembered what his father told him the other night, when he came back from washing his hands and putting iodine on the cuts.

"It wasn't right to do that, Chuck—turn in that alarm, but it wasn't exactly wrong either."

"Yes, sir."

"I don't want you to call me sir, Chuck. I'm dad. Dad."

"Yes, dad."

"You see, actually it's against the law to turn in an alarm. You know that. It puts folks to a lot of trouble. The firemen. It costs the taxpayer a lot of money."

"Yes, dad."

"I know why you did it. I was a kid once myself, you know. I know why you did it."

"You *do*, dad?"

"Sure, Chuck."

"Why?"

"What?"

"Why did I do it?"

"Well, because you're a boy. It's a boy's prank. Once when Howie was your age, he let air out of all the tires on the cars parked down on Easton Street. It's that kind of thing."

"Yes, dad."

"Isn't it? You wanted to have some fun. Hmmm?"

"I guess so."

"You see, it may seem like fun, but it causes a lot of trouble."

"I'm sorry, dad."

"It's nothing to go down in the dumps about. You've been under a lot of pressure. All that television and *Life* magazine. It's got under your skin. Your mother should know that."

"Dad?"

"Yes, Chuck?"

"You won't have a disagreement with her about it?"

"You see, there you go again."

"I'm sorry. You won't fight with her?"

"I'm not going to fight with her. But I'm not going to let her get on your back about it either."

"I don't mind."

"There's no reason for her to shout at you. You've been under pressure. And another thing, Chuck."

"Yes, dad?"

"About what you said to your mother, you know—about the dictionary?"

"I said masticate, dad."

"Hell, I know what you said! There's no reason to repeat it. I'm just trying to tell you in a nice way that a boy keeps those things to himself."

"It's a misunderstanding, sir. I said—"

"Don't sir me, Chuck. Didn't I ask you not to sir me?"

"Yes, sir, dad. Yes, dad."

"Now we'll just forget about it. Everyone has a right to privacy. Just keep that stuff private, Chuck."

"All right."

"I was a boy once myself, you know. I know a little bit about my own kid," said his father, smiling. "Don't you let your mother tell you it'll make you crazy either. She tried to tell Howie that. Women don't understand, Chuck."

"I see."

"She'd like it if you were Little Lord Fauntleroy, I guess."

"Who?"

"Oh, some kid sissy that used to be in the movies. You wouldn't remember."

"You mean in that novel by Frances Hodgson Burnett, written in 1886?"

"Chuck, why do you have to sound off about everything? Can't you let anything go by? You're not on Cash-Answer now. You're in your bedroom, having a little 'confab' with your dad. You don't have to sound off on everything under the sun."

"I just wanted you to know I knew who Lord Fauntleroy was. I remembered just after you said it."

"I wouldn't care if you didn't know who he was. I'd like it a lot better if you *didn't* know something for a change."

"I'm sorry, dad."

"And stop apologizing all the time. You don't have to apologize. It's a free country."

"Yes, dad."

"We'll play some ball tomorrow, want to?"

"Yes. I want to."

"We'll make out okay, Chuck, you and me. You just try to get a grip on yourself and not think you have to know all the answers. Okay?"

"Certainly. I mean, okay, dad!"

"Now, go on to sleep," said his father.

"All right."

"Well, what are you doing over there?"

"Just checking my rack, dad."

"There's nothing wrong with your rack. I told you time and time again. Those knives aren't going to fall out of there."

"I'm sorry."

"You don't have to be sorry. I only want you to know this rack is secure," said his father. He slapped the rack with his palm. "See? It's secure."

"I see."

"And anyway, what if a knife did come out of there? What would it hurt?"

"I don't know."

"It'd just fall on the floor."

"Yes, I see."

"Get a good night's sleep, son."

"Thank you, dad."

"We'll play some ball out behind the house tomorrow!"

Charles Berrey sat at the dining room table, sipping his soup and going over the conversation with his father in his mind. He believed he had devised a plan that would *really* please his father. It might put an end to all the arguing between his mother and father as well. It was a very simple plan, inspired by what his father had said about not knowing all the answers all the time. Next week on Cash-Answer, he would give the wrong answer to the question Jackie Paul asked him. He would miss.

Then everything would get back to normal. His father would go back on the road, and there would be no more arguments. That way, he wouldn't be a quiz kid any longer. But neither would he have to catch fly balls out behind the house until his palms ached. In a gesture of sudden resolve, Charles Berrey bit into his egg and olive sandwich, and began masticating it.

PART FOUR

Chapter Ten

BROCK BROWN

It was Memorial Day eve. At six o'clock it began to rain. Brock pushed his coat sleeve back with his fingers to see the time. He sighed, leaned over and took the keys from the ignition and put them in his pocket. Then he rested his elbows on the steering wheel and watched the raindrops dribble down the windshield.

"You can't blame me for being surprised," said Carrie Bates. "I guess everyone in Murray's was surprised."

She sat beside him in the front seat of his car, her books on her lap, her long fingers with the blood-colored nails, playing with the charms on a gold bracelet she wore around her arm. Her long black hair spilled shining to her shoulders. She was wearing a black sweater, a black skirt, and a black sweater-jacket, with black socks and loafers that were a dark brown color. Brock wondered why she had not tried for more contrast—a white sweater, maybe, or a yellow one, with matching socks. He was wearing sky blue against navy, no other colors.

"I'm glad you asked to drive me home," she said. "I've always wanted to get to know you better. You're hard to know, Brock."

"I've been out this way two or three times before," said he.

"By yourself?"

"Sure."

101

"That's what I mean about you. Way out in the country by yourself. You're a lone wolf or something."

He said, "Are you going away too?"

"What do you mean?"

"For the weekend? Memorial Day? Clara and my father left this noon."

"Yes, we're going tonight. Daddy likes to drive late at night. Besides," she laughed, "Mother wouldn't miss Cash-Answer. Do you watch it?"

"Sometimes."

"Well, what do you *do*, Brock?"

"I stay out of trouble. Nothing special."

"You're a funny guy."

"I'm all shook up."

She gave a whoop of laughter. "All shook up," she said. "That's a riot!"

"I *am*."

"You don't know how much of a riot it is to hear *you* talk like that."

"Why not *me*?"

"I don't know."

"Boy cat, all shook up."

She laughed again.

Then there was silence for awhile. She continued to pull at the charms on her bracelet, and Brock sat in the same position—his elbows resting on the steering wheel. She was beginning to get restless now. She couldn't figure him out at all. When he had walked over to her, back in Murray's, she had thought it would be the start of something crazy and beautiful and wonderful. Leaving like that with him, while Derby Wylie and everyone gaped after them with unabashed, wide-eyed amazement, Carrie Bates had visualized a succession of fabulous scenes-to-come: Brock and she swimming out at the quarry this summer, while the crowd lolled around on multi-colored beach towels, watching them, whispering; Brock and she whipping past them in his convertible, her long black hair flying in the wind, he, in sunglasses—immaculate, handsome, mysterious to everyone but her; the two of them dancing in a dark corner under the Japanese lanterns at the Sykes High prom; the pair of them sitting in the back booth in the rear of Murray's, involved in an intensely serious conversation —scene after scene after scene, Carrie and Brock. . . . But

on their way out here to this back-country road, he had
said practically nothing; and now?

"You have a good roof," she said, touching the top of
the convertible with her fingers. "It doesn't leak in the
rain."

"I watched Cash-Answer just last week," he said. "It
doesn't seem a week."

"My mother's crazy about that little eight-year-old."

"Time fugits," he said, sighing. He leaned back. "Tem-
pus flys."

"Brock?"

"What?"

"Speaking of time . . . I have some packing to do before
dinner. We ought to start back."

"Where are you and your folks going, anyway?"

"Just to Rochester. My uncle lives there."

"Clara and my father went to the Adirondacks."

"Hadn't we ought to start back?"

"Well . . . Well, it's a long way back."
She laughed. "I guess we'll make it."

"I always have."

"Is anything—bothering you, Brock?"

"I'm all shook up," he said.

Again she laughed, but for the first time, she was beginning to wonder if there wasn't something wrong with
him. What had he brought her way out here for anyway?
Just to mope around?

"Everything makes you laugh, doesn't it, Carrie?" he
said.

"Not everything. I just can't figure you out."

"I had a little talk with the head-shrinker a couple of
days back. He couldn't either."

"Who?"

"Mannerheim. Ye old head-shrinker."

"He's not a real head-shrinker. He just teaches it."

"He'd like to get me into trouble, I think."

"Brock, do you know that it's after six?"

"It isn't my fault that it's raining, Carrie. You can
blame a lot of things on me, but not the weather,
for Pete's sake."

"I'm not blaming anything on you. But I have to get
back. We eat at seven, and I have to pack before dinner."

"Go ahead then. Go ahead."

"I'm suppose to walk back, I suppose!"

"I'll walk with you, when the rain stops," said he. "There's no sense getting soaked."

"Walk! Oh, come on, Brock. I'm not joking."

"I'm not either."

"Are we out of gas or something?"

"There's nothing wrong with the car. It's after six."

"So what?"

"Im not supposed to drive after six, Carrie. That's the law. I'm only a Junior Operator."

"Brock, are you out of your mind?"

"Do you think I'm going to break the law?"

"Do you think *I'm* going to *walk* home?"

"We'll try to get a ride. When it stops raining, I'll help you."

"Brock Brown, you take me home! Right now!"

"I'm not going to get soaked to the skin! Are you kidding?" said the boy. "Look at that road! Mud!"

"You're crazy! You're crazy!"

"Shook up! All shook up, Carrie."

"I will get out of here! I'll get out of here right now!" She slammed her hand down on the handle of the Chevy's door, opening it. "You'll hear from my father, Brock Brown!"

"You're behaving like a child, Carrie."

"You—*nut!*" she said.

She left the door of the car open and disappeared behind the car. Brock Brown reached out quickly, catching the handle and pulling the door closed before any more rain dribbled onto the slip covers.

For a moment, he saw Carrie in his rear-view mirror, going along in the rain, carrying her books under her arm. Then she veered sharply to the right, out of the mirror's range. Brock sat back, shaking. It was all right now. It was going to be all right. She was gone.

The rain had been like a miracle. It had come to clean the dirty thoughts out of his mind. If it hadn't rained, he might be right out there now, in the fields with her, walking right into Mannerheim's trap. He had known on the drive out that he was not that kind of guy. The moment she had gotten inside of his car, he had known that, but he would have tried, if it had not been for the rain. One thing disappointed him terribly. It was the way she had reacted when he told her that he was not going to break

the law. She had said: Do you think I'm going to *walk*
home? What if it hadn't rained? Would she have still
said that, still not cared one damn that he was not the
kind of guy who broke laws? If so, she was worse than he
had ever imagined.

What if it hadn't rained? That was one thing he hadn't
counted on.

He had planned to say, "Well, Carrie, it's after six
o'clock. You know what that means. I can't drive the car
any more."

"I know," she might have said. "Something told me
you'd be the kind of fellow that would respect the law."

"How'd you know that?"

"Well," she might have said, "my mother knew your
mother. You're a Brock, after all."

"That's all right, Carrie. Don't worry about it. I'll hike
a ride out here tomorrow and pick up the car."

"You don't mind, Brock?" she might have said.

"Come on, Carrie. I'll take the books. We'll get a ride
on the highway."

"You're a wonderful guy, Brock. A wonderful guy!"

And then? Even then, even if everything had worked
out according to plan, Brock wondered if he could have
gone through with it.

"It's a beautiful day, Brock."

"It's almost night, Carrie."

"But it isn't dark."

*"No, it isn't. Do you think I would have brought you
out here in the dark? You've got the wrong fellow,
Carrie."*

*"I know that. I know you wouldn't have. Let's sit down
here in the fields, for a minute, Brock."*

*"It's clean out here, Carrie. Good clean air, and not
even dark."*

"I knew you weren't like the others."

*"I'm not perverse, Carrie. But I'm not Derby Wylie's
kind either."*

Still, there would have been the dirty pictures in his
mind. What was wrong with a girl like Carrie Bates, anyway? You just had to walk up to her in Murray's and
wham-o! What if her mother knew about her? That
would be something, if Mrs. Bates knew. In the car on

the drive out, the first thing Carrie had tried to do was to get some of that rock 'n' roll on the radio. At least he had taught her that much.

"I don't like bad music," he had said.

She said, "Brock Brown, you went roaring out of the parking lot just the other afternoon, with that kind of music playing loud as a band!"

"I realized my mistake. I turned it off. Don't worry about me."

"You're funny," she said.

"Anyone can make a mistake," he told her.

It was all right now. When the rain stopped, Brock would walk to the highway and get a ride back home. He had the whole weekend to himself—three days!

His hand was in the pocket of his navy blue jacket. His fingers felt the key there. He remembered something Clara said to him that noon, before she and his father left. It was vile!

"Well, keep your nose clean, Brock!" she had said.

It was one of the dirtiest things anyone had ever said to him.

What kind of a world was it anyway? There was Mannerheim telling him to do dirty things to girls or he would be a pervert, and there was Clara talking that way about snot (she might just as well have said the word right out!), and then Carrie, not caring if he broke the law, not respecting him because he would not drive after six.

Why didn't he throw the key away? What did he want with the Rubins' key? He wasn't a goddam Nazi or something. He even liked Mrs. Rubin, even though her flower pots did leak. Throw the key away, then. Throw the key away, he thought.

Brock Brown sat there like that in his car, in the rain. When the door on his side opened suddenly, he was startled.

"I am *not* going to walk home! You take me home!"

Carrie Bates looked odd with her hair wet and stringy, with rain dripping off her nose.

He said, "If you want to wait until the rain stops, I have some tarpaulin in the back seat."

It would still be all right. Even if the rain stopped, everything was too wet now. But he wished she hadn't come back like this. He was tired of her now. He didn't want Carrie Bates for anything.

She said, "You put your car keys in and take me home, right now."

"Go around to the other door and get in the back," he said. "When the rain stops, we'll get a ride."

"You're not crazy! You're just plain stupid! You're a stupid nut! Now, come on, Brock!"

"Carrie, I'm not going to break the law for you or anyone else. Now, get in back. Look what you're doing to the seat. Shut that door, and go around and get in back!"

He didn't even realize what was happening then. Carrie Bates bent over and scooped up mud from the road. She brought her hand up to his face, and pushed the mud down it, across his nose and his chin, down to the powder blue short-sleeve shirt he wore under his jacket. There was wet mud all over him. For a moment he simply sat there, realizing this. Then suddenly, he leapt from the car and caught ahold of her. Her books slipped from her arm. He pushed her backward, and she fell screaming to the dirt road. Brock fell on top of her.

"Don't!" she said, "Please!" she said.

But it was too late. There was no headache this time. There was something far more immediate and demanding. He struggled with her there in the mud, with the rain pouring down on them. His thumbs finally found her neck, pressing against it until she was still . . . Later, he took his jackknife from his trousers pocket.

After, when Brock Brown tried to run, he kept slipping and sliding and falling to his knees. "Like a little pig!" he said aloud, "God, like a little pig!"

He sat down in the mud, holding the jackknife in his hand. He looked ahead of him at his car, parked there with the door open and the rain getting the slipcovers wet. He looked at himself; light against dark, navy and light blue, but he was filthy now, and wet, and there was another color—blood red. Very carefully, he reached in his pocket for two things—the handkerchief and the Rubins' key. With a smile, he threw the key away. Then he wrapped the knife in the handkerchief and put it back in his pocket. The police would want the knife. It was evidence, and it was against the law to withhold evidence. His smile broke to laughter, and his laughter gave away to deep, shaking sobs . . . Boy cat, all shook up . . . Boy cat, all shook up.

Chapter Eleven

REGINALD WHITTIER

"I'll be right with you," said Laura Lee Whittier. "I just have to serve a ham and eggs at Number 3."

In the diner, the television set was on. There were half-a-dozen people at the counter, lingering over coffee and hamburgers, waiting for Cash-Answer to begin.

Reginald Whittier walked to a booth in the rear. Laura had gotten the job here two days ago, the same day the doctor had verified her pregnancy. Yesterday morning, there had been further verification. Seeing his wife sick like that had made Reggie ill himself. Laura had borrowed some Alka-Seltzer from the landlady and fixed it for him before she went off to work.

"Just take it easy," she told him. "You'll feel better. Just rest awhile—and honey, rest in the bed. Not on the floor. After all, *I* can't bite you or anything. I'll be at work."

"I'm going to find work too," he said. "I'll have a job by the time I pick you up tonight."

Reggie sat down in the booth and lit a cigarette. He inhaled the smoke, thinking of the way she had taught him to do that, thinking of all the patience she had, only vaguely interested in the face of the eight-year-old on the television screen, or the voice of the quizmaster.

"Back tonight for his fourth appearance on CASH-ANSWER is young, eight-year-old Charles Berrey, from Reddton, New Jersey!"

Laura appeared with a cup of coffee, setting it in front of him, sitting down beside him.

"I can't stay along," she said, "but you can watch the television. I'll only be another half-hour."

"Has it been busy?"

"Murder! Jeez!"

"I'm sorry about flaring up earlier, Laur. I didn't mean to."

108

"Aw, honey, you're just nervous. It made me nervous to job-hunt too."

"I really tried today, Laur. I just can't seem to get anywhere."

"It's hard without experience."

"I start stuttering. I *know* that's it. I can't get a word out."

"If you'd only let me teach you how to carry a tray, Reg. Honestly, it's the simplest thing in the world. You just get the palm of your right hand smack under the middle of the tray, see, and—"

"I can't be a waiter, Laura! It isn't carrying the trays that bothers me. I just can't do that work. Sales or something. I could do what I did at Whittier's Wheel."

"Which was *what*, exactly?"

"*You* know!"

"Reggie, I'm not hopping on you or anything, but there just aren't jobs like that. Now if you could wait table or something, you could make up experience. And you could start right away."

"I'll think of something."

"You just can't *think* of something. You have to *do* something."

"I know it! I know that!"

"Oh gosh, there's Number 3 looking for me . . . Don't worry, honey," she said standing up, "it'll work out."

"I hope so."

"Hey, here's the letter from my mom." She reached in her pocket and handed it to him. "Read it. I'll be back in a sec."

Reggie took another drag from his cigarette and removed the letter from the envelope. He sipped the coffee and began reading:

Dear, Laura,

Well that was some surprise running off that way but I guess you know what your doing by now, your pa is not to mad but I guess it gave him a jolt so he has not much to say on the subjick, and anyway we are very busy with the colledge getting ready for the parants day and graduashun coming on its way, bye bye and let us know more about this boy as I guess he's in the family when you come right down to it, love and kisses, ma.

Reggie squashed out the cigarette in the ashtray and shoved the letter in his pocket. Still no word from *his* mother. It was too early. He had only mailed the postcard yesterday, but it was strange she had done nothing to find him. She would only have to report the car's theft, if she had really wanted to locate him. Could there be anything wrong? Could she be ill or anything? He thought of the letter Laura's mother had sent her, and of what his own mother would have said about it. Tobacco Road. Itinerant workers. Showed up, all right. . . . He didn't mean that. He didn't want to think things like that. It was just that everything was so different now. Here he was married, with a pregnant wife who wanted him to be a waiter, and the two of them living in a tourist home. He had to come to a diner to watch television. He wondered vaguely if his mother were watching Cash-Answer now, if she were seeing the same thing he saw on the big television set up front—the kid going into the Contemplation Chamber, the camera moving in for a close-up of him with the earphones over his head. He looked like a little bug.

Laura was back. She squeezed in beside him. "Did you like mom's letter, Reggie?"

"Yes," he said.

"She's awful nice about everything, isn't she?"

"Sure, I suppose so."

"What do you mean by that?"

"Wait until she finds out you're pregnant."

"I'm not going to tell her. At least not yet. I'll just wait awhile, and then tell her. She won't even know the difference."

"She can count, can't she, Laur?"

"Lots of people have premature babies."

"I wouldn't know."

"Sure, honey. The period of gestation differs with women."

"Gestation, ovulation—you know all *those* big words."

"A girl has to. I read up in medical books."

"Okay! Okay!"

"Why do you get so touchy when I talk about it?"

"Laur, you don't have to talk about it all the time. That's all."

"I hardly ever talk about it."

"You've been talking about it for months. All about

taking your temperature, and ovulation—that's all you've been talking about."

"Oh, come on, Reggie! Gee, that just *isn't* true—"

"Listen!" he said, "The quiz kid's on."

"I hardly ever talk about it," she said.

They sat there side by side in Mac's Diner, staring up at the television screen. Reggie lit another cigarette and sat back with a sigh.

". . . *have only one chance to identify these American butterflies, Chuck, so be careful not to blurt out your answers too quickly. Take your time. Study the pictures in front of you. And for $52,000, tell me the answers to this question. Can you hear me all right, Chuck?*"

"*Yes, sir. I mean, Jackie.*"

"*About sixty species make up the nymphs and satyrs. About two thousand species make up the coppers and blues. The largest species—the swallowtails—have over twenty species native to America. Using the pictures you are holding in your hands, name the butterfly family, the species, and the locale where this species is most commonly found in the United States. Do you understand the question, Chuck?*"

"*Yes, I understand.*"

"*Start with picture Number 1.*"

"*That's a common wood nymph. From the South and Southwestern parts of the United States.*"

"*That's correct for Number 1.*"

"I'm sorry," said Reggie Whittier to his wife. "Maybe you *don't* talk about it all the time."

"You're nice, Reggie. Do you know that?"

"I don't like to pick on you all the time, Laura."

"I don't mind. When you apologize like that, I want to cry or something."

"This kid knows plenty, doesn't he?"

"I mean it, Reggie. I think you're a swell husband."

"Thanks."

"*Picture Number 4, now, Chuck. Do you have it?*"

"*Yes.*"

"*Take as much time as you can, Chuck.*"

"*Number 4 is a blue. A pigmy blue. Common to the West.*"

"*Right again, Chuck. Now, Number 5.*"

"Oh, oh, someone wants their check. I'll be right back."

"Okay, Laur."

"Don't go away," she said. "I'll only be a sec."

"*Would you repeat that, Chuck. Number 5 is what?*"

"*He's a tiger swallowtail.*"

"*Chuck—Chuck, I'm sorry fellow. I'm sorry, Chuck. Gee, this is too bad, fellow. It says here on my card that Number 5 is a zebra swallowtail, fellow.*"

"*I'm sorry.*"

"*Gosh, Chuck, I'm the guy who's sorry. All perfect answers but Number 5. I guess that's it, Chuck. You want to step out of the Contemplation Chamber, please?*"

Some of the people at the counter groaned.

The studio audience applauded wildly as the eight-year-old on the television screen came out of the booth.

A woman in front of Reginald Whittier said, "That doesn't seem fair! He knew all but one!"

Another woman shushed her.

"*Well, Chuck, you don't go home empty-handed. You still get all 32 volumes of the Encyclopaedia Britannica.*"

"*Yes, sir.*"

"*That was a rough deal, wasn't it, Chuck. But now there'll be more time for baseball.*"

"*Yes, there will be.*"

"*Still going to be a ballplayer when you grow up?*"

"*That's right.*"

"*Well, Chuck, no one here doubts that whatever you decide to be, you'll be good at it.*"

"*Thank you.*"

"*How about that, folks?*"

The studio audience applauded a second time. So did the lady sitting at the booth in front of Reggie Whittier.

Now the quizmaster was welcoming another contestant. A minister, whose category was famous hymns.

"I just have to get my apron off, Reg," Laura said as she passed by. "I'll only be a sec."

It was beginning to get on his nerves the way she always said "a sec." He wondered why he was sitting there kidding himself. It would never work out. Nothing ever had. Everything he had tried to do on his own, from the Boy Scout Jamboree when he was thirteen to *this,* had been a huge flop. He thought of the way he had cut his face shaving that morning. He had been standing there in the room at the tourist home looking into the mirror, and in the mirror's reflection, he had seen Laura's things again, hanging up all over the place; hanging up to dry—stockings and the panties she had bought yesterday from her advance in salary, and the slip. She had gone to work.

"I just won't wear a slip," she had said before she left. "I'm not going to spend good money on a new slip, and this one's not dry. I have to buy a new garter belt, though. The elastic's gone on the one I'm wearing."

He hadn't wanted to hear all that. Why did she have to talk about it all the time? Through all the years of living with his mother, he had never once heard her mention anything about her underclothing.

He stood there shaving, thinking about it, and he cut his upper lip.

Now, he was smoking all the time too. One right after the other. He ground out his cigarette and finished his coffee.

"All right, Reverend Handson, for $44,000 answer this question. A famous hymn will play in just one second. You are to give me the name of the hymn, the name of the man who wrote words of the hymn, the year he wrote the hymn, the name of a novel he wrote, and the name of the man who wrote the music of this hymn."

"I'm ready, Mr. Paul."

"Listen carefully to this famous hymn!"

When the music began, the woman in the booth in front of Reggie said, "Why, that's easy! Who doesn't know that hymn?"

"Sure, but who wrote it, smarty?" another woman in the diner said, "and what year? Hah?"

The sound of the martial music filled the diner.

Reggie began to tremble. He noticed his hands shake as he reached for the cup of coffee in front of him. The cup was empty.

He wanted to get out of there suddenly, away from the sound of the music. He sat frozen, wanting to go, unable to move.

Then ·he heard Laura's voice behind him. "Hey, Reggie. Your mother wants you!"

He whirled around, "What? What?"

She was laughing at him. "That's her signal, isn't it, honey?"

He wanted to hit her. He wanted to slap her face for saying that. He got up and stood there, facing her.

"What's the matter?" she said.

People were watching them. Reggie could feel their eyes on him.

His face was hot and red. He wanted to shout at her to be quiet.

"I was making a joke," she said, "You know how your mother always played that—"

He raised his fist. He shook it at her. "You just sh-sh-sh-sh—" He couldn't get the words out. Again, he tried, "Sh-sh-sh—"

Laura simply stood there with that hurt expression in her eyes.

Then someone else said the words he couldn't say. The woman in front of Reggie. He stared at her.

"You shut up," she said. "You just shut up and listen!"

Reginald Whittier sat back down in the booth. He put his head in the cradle of his arms, on the table. Goose bumps came out all over him. He began to shake, without crying.

Sabine Baring-Gould wrote that hymn, Mr. Paul, in the year 1865. Sir Arthur Sullivan set it to music. Sabine Baring-Gould also wrote a novel called The Broom Squire. *I guess there's not a living soul who doesn't know that the name of that hymn is "Onward, Christian Soldiers."*

Then there were bells ringing and there was the thunder of applause. Reggie looked up at the television set while the drums beat, and the lights on the ˉContemplation Chamber blinked on and off.

"Sh-sh-sh-shut up!" Reggie Whittier whispered, and the tears started streaming down his face.

Chapter Twelve

CHARLES BERREY

Before they got into the elevator at International Broadcasting Company, Evelyn Berrey said: "Leave him alone, Howard!"

"I'd just like an answer to my question, Evelyn. This is *one* question the boy can answer. Now how about it, Chuck?"

"The elevator's here now. Ask him, later."

"Chuck?" said Howard Berrey, "Are you going to answer me?"

"Here, dad?" Did his father want him to say it right in front of his mother?

"Yes, here."

"All right, dad. I *was* spoofing."

"I knew it! I knew it!"

"Chuckles, *are you serious?"*

The elevator boy shouted: "Down! Down car!"

"Anyone knows a zebra swallowtail," said Charles Berrey.

He looked up at his father and smiled broadly.

"You damn little brat!" said his father between his teeth, "You goddam little brat!" He caught a hold of the boy's collar and shoved him toward the elevator.

"Be careful, Howard!" said Evelyn Berrey. "Don't lose your temper here. Don't talk in the elevator!"

The elevator boy touched his finger to his cap.

"Hi, folks. Tough luck, Chuck. Better luck next time."

"Thank you," said Charles Berrey.

His father looked down at him with angry eyes. Under his breath, he said: "Only there won't *be* a next time."

"I thought it would be all right, dad. I thought—"

"Chuckles," his mother interrupted him. "Button up your coat, and wait until we're in the car if you have anything to tell your father."

"Yes, Chuckles," said his father, with that mocking tone of mimicry, "button up your lip *too,* for now!"

115

Charles Berrey saw his mother shove her elbow in his father's side. The elevator was zooming down to the first floor of I.B.C. Charles could feel it in his ears. They felt as though they would pop. He stood between his parents nervously, while no one said another thing.

On one, the elevator doors shot open.

"Goodnight, folks."

Charles turned around to wave at the elevator boy, but his mother grabbed his hand, and yanked him along a few steps ahead of his father.

"Chuckles, your father is very, very angry!"

"I thought it would be all right. I thought he—"

"Don't hang to your *mother's* skirts," said Howard Berrey as he caught up with them. "We'll just have a little 'confab' about this, mister! Later!"

"It was a silly thing to do, Chuckles. All that money."

"I have to work ten years to make that much money!" said his father, "and you just throw it away!"

As they approached the entranceway of I.B.C., half-a-dozen reporters stood waiting.

"Give us a big smile, Chuck!" said one, as the flash bulb on his Graflex sparked.

Howard Berrey said, "We have no comment."

"How about that, Chuck?" another reporter asked.

"Please," said Mrs. Berrey, "Chuckles is tired."

"Is that your pet name for him, Mrs. Berrey?"

"Did the boy have a temporary lapse of memory, or was it a real miss?"

"Mr. Berrey, are you glad the ordeal is over?"

The reporters stood in a circle around the Berrey's. More flash bulbs exploded, and more questions were fired at the trio.

Suddenly, Howard Berrey shoved his son in front of him.

"Go ahead, Chuck. Tell them."

Charles Berrey said, "I knew it was a zebra swallowtail."

"He knew the answer," said Evelyn Berrey.

The reporter with the Graflex said, "Didn't they give you enough time, Chuck? Did you feel pressed for time?"

"No," said Charles Berrey. "I knew instantly."

"Tell them, Chuck," said Howard Berrey.

Charles Berrey's lips were trembling now.

"What do you mean you knew instantly?" said another reporter. "Were you just nervous?"

"Answer them, Chuck!" his father demanded.

"Howard! After all—" said Evelyn Berrey.

"Chuck, did you *hear* me?"

"I was—I was spoofing," said Charles Berrey.

"You mean that you knew the answer, and gave the wrong answer?"

"Yes, sir," he told the reporter. "Anyone knows a zebra swallowtail."

Another flash bulb exploded.

"Why?" said a reporter.

"Why did you give the wrong answer, Chuck?"

"Are you spoofing now, Chuck?" said the man with the Graflex.

"Why?" the first reporter repeated his question.

Charles Berrey stood there in front of his father, biting his lip and staring up at them.

"Do you know why you did it, Chuck?"

"Why, Chuck?"

"Did anyone tell you to do it, Chuck? Was it fixed?"

"Why, Chuck?"

"Why, boy?"

Howard Berrey grabbed his son's arm. "No comment," he said.

"We just want some peace," said Evelyn Berrey.

"Do you believe your son?" asked the man with the Graflex. "Mr. Berrey, do you believe your son was spoofing?"

Howard Berrey turned and glared at the reporter. "You're goddam right I believe him!" he said.

Then he yanked Charles by the arm and pushed his way through the revolving door.

Momentarily, Evelyn Berrey lingered before the reporters.

"What about it, Mrs. Berrey?"

"Do you believe him too, Mrs. Berrey?"

"Chuckles didn't mean to do it. I don't even think he realized what he was doing," she mumbled. "You see, it was sort of a game to him."

"Are you mad at him, Mrs. Berrey? Are you and your husband mad at him?"

But she didn't answer. She pushed her way through the revolving door with the dazed expression of somebody who had just lost a fortune and wasn't yet able to quite believe it.

PART FIVE

PART FIVE

PART SIX

Chapter Sixteen

BROCK BROWN

It was Saturday morning, the day after Memorial Day.
In the corridor of the Kantogee County Children's
Home, where Brock was being held, Robert Brown faced
the psychiatrist the circuit judge had appointed to examine the boy.

"Of course," said Dr. Baird, "my opinion isn't the only
one that counts in a case like this. After all, there's the
hearing on the petition asking the juvenile waiver, and
there are still some mental tests we want to give Brock."

"They'll try him for homicide if you say he's sane," said
Robert Brown. "I'm sure of that."

"I'm sorry, Mr. Brown. I have to do my duty the way
I see it."

"He *must* have been insane, doctor. You said yourself
there was that business about his mother, about his thinking he was responsible for her death."

"Mr. Brown, I said there was a good possibility that
Brock felt *some* responsibility because he may have wished
her dead."

"You never knew my wife, doctor. She hated that boy."

"I never knew either one of you, Mr. Brown. If your
son did wish his mother dead, and felt guilty as a result, it
may certainly have contributed to a neurosis. That was
probably why he felt sex was evil. Your wife died in childbirth. But a neurosis of that sort is quite common. Many

141

children wish their parents were dead, and parents die every day."

"Explain to me about his obsession with dirt again. Could you just do that, doctor?"

"Mr. Brown, a child soils. A child is always soiling, one way or the other. His mother must have blamed Brock for being dirty."

"She used to call him a little pig, doctor!"

"Then, of course, you were a mechanic. There was always dirt on your clothes. Your wife may have mentioned that when the boy could hear it. Or perhaps the boy imagined that she did. Dirt symbolized blame to your son, and it also may well have symbolized sex, the thing that killed your wife."

"Do you call that sane?" said Robert Brown.

"Mr. Brown, this is very unnecessary—all of it. I told you before, and I'm very sorry that I have to repeat it: in my opinion your son knows the difference between right and wrong. He is also capable of understanding the court proceeding against him, should that be the case, and of helping in his own defense."

"Dr. Baird, listen. Please. I don't understand this. I wish I could talk with you, or Dr. Fletcher. Won't you explain it to me?"

"Dr. Fletcher agrees with my diagnosis, Mr. Brown. Now, neither of *us* is on trial."

"It's just that I want to help my boy."

"And I wish I could help you, Mr. Brown. But there's absolutely nothing more I can do."

The doctor touched his hand to his hat as he placed it on his head and went back down the corridor.

Momentarily, Robert Brown stood watching him go. Then slowly he turned and went toward the room where Brock was waiting for him.

"Hello, son," he said as the guard shut the door behind them.

Brock smiled meekly, standing to greet his father.

"Hello, dad."

"I brought the clothes you wanted. I gave them to Officer Raleigh."

"Thank you."

"Clara sends her love, son."

"I suppose *she's* mad."

"Why do you say that, Brock? There's no one mad."

"She had to come back from her vacation, didn't she?"

"Brock, we're not thinking about a vacation or anything else but how to help you."

"Me? I'm helpless."

"No one is helpless when people care about them."

"I guess you can have more children, dad. I'm glad of that. Clara wants a baby."

"Right now, Clara and I want *you*, Brock."

"Do you, dad?"

The boy began to cry. He sat down in the leather chair in the anteroom and held his head with his hands. "I don't know why it happened. I've tried and tried to figure it out. The doctors were here, the head-shrinkers. They know why, I suppose. I suppose they can figure the whole thing out, just like they always do. They think they know everything!"

"They think you're sane, Brock."

"I am! I told them I was!"

"You couldn't have been, Brock. I know my own kid, don't I? Something must have gone wrong in your mind."

"No, dad. That's where you're wrong. Listen, dad. I'll tell you something," the boy said. "Earlier in the day— earlier, I was worried. I thought something might go wrong. I was all shook up, anway. Remember last night I told you that it was really me who took that flowerpot?"

"You never explained why."

"I had a headache, dad. I had to take it. I don't know. But that's nothing. Dad, I took something else."

"Something else?"

"A key, dad. I took a key that night when the Rubins called you up and made you and Clara come over. It was a key to their house, dad. I'm sure it was."

"But why? Why did you do that?"

"I don't know. I had a funny feeling about that key. That I was going to use it for something."

"For what, son? For what?"

"Something! I don't know! That's how come I know I'm sane. All day I was thinking of using the key. I wanted to go back there to the Rubins. I wanted—to get them."

"Get them for what? Sam and Estelle Rubin?"

"That flowerpot leaked all over me. It made me mad. I couldn't forget it, dad. I kept that key. I was so afraid I almost told one of the teachers at school about it. But I didn't. I just kept it. In my pocket."

"I don't understand, Brock. Sam and Estelle Rubin never did anything to you."

"I know it. That was what was so crazy! But dad—listen, after Carrie—after what I did, dad, I didn't want the key any more."

"What do you mean, Brock? I'm trying to understand."

"I didn't want the key any more, dad! I threw it away! I felt silly carrying that key around! Don't you see? I didn't want it!"

"I'm trying to see, Brock—I'm trying."

"Dad, if I was insane, I would have wanted to keep that key! I would have wanted to do something with it. I don't even know *what*, for Pete's sake! Don't you get it?"

"Son, son, I'm trying to understand."

"It was just like when I took the Mercury last week. After I tied the ten dollars to the steering wheel. I didn't want that car! I didn't want it! I felt silly! Just like when I knew I didn't want the key any more."

Robert Brown stood there staring at his son, a look of incredulousness on his face. He was beginning to remember something—beginning to remember the day last week when he had gotten the call at the garage to pick up an abandoned car.

"Was it a green Mercury, Brock?" he said. "It wasn't a *green* Mercury?"

It had been left on a back-country road, with ten dollars held to the chrome steering wheel by a rubber band . . . It had been left on a dirt road . . . the same dirt road near Eastern Highway and Simon Point.

"Yes," said Robert Brown's son, grinning, "it *was* green. How did *you* know, dad?"

Chapter Seventeen

CHARLES BERREY

QUIZ KID TURNS FIRE-BUG, 1 DEAD

Quiz kid Charles Berrey, known to television viewers as "Chuck," the bespectacled, eight-year-old with the elephantine memory, formerly a contestant on Cash-Answer, set fire to the library in his home town on Memorial Day afternoon.

Overcome by smoke and unable to escape a flaming death was Reddton's beloved librarian, Miss Margaret Schuster.

The blaze was set at approximately four forty-five, while citizens of Reddton paid solemn tribute to the war dead in the lobby of the library. There, Miss Schuster had arranged an exhibit tracing the history of the Unknown Soldier in this country.

Charles Berrey, questioned on the lawn of the library while firemen were inside attempting to quell the flames, confessed to setting the fire. He said that he began the blaze with a newspaper in the library's basement, where he had been "thinking."

Just what this boy-genius with ambitions to be a baseball player was "thinking" to compel him to arson he refused to make clear. Spectators alleged that the boy's failure to answer a question on the television show Cash-Answer Memorial Day eve may have incited his resentment against this building, which housed so much information on so many subjects.

The small, nervous youngster, described by neighbors as "more of a bookworm than a ball-player," forfeited $52,000 when he incorrectly identified a zebra swallowtail butterfly as a tiger swallowtail. After the television show, he made the tearful, unconvincing claim that he had known the correct answer "instantly," that he had been merely "spoofing."

A witness to this scene in the International Broadcasting Company building alleged that the father of the boy, Howard Berrey, salesman, had obviously forced his son to tell this falsehood.

"It was plain that the father was embarrassed and outraged at the kid's failure," the witness stated. "The kid was a wreck when he left I.B.C!"

Miss Margaret Schuster, age 59, could have escaped death had she not attempted to rescue the boy. Known as "Chuckles" to his family, the frail child apparently became fearful once the fire was underway in the Children's Section of the library. He called to Miss Schuster, who immediately ran down the stairs to see what had happened.

"I tried to warn her to run," said the boy, "but she was pulling at the fire extinguisher and telling me to get out of the building. There was smoke everywhere. I couldn't see her any more. I ran up the stairs calling, 'Fire! Fire!' "

One man was burned in a futile attempt to go after the librarian, and several others were driven back by smoke and flames.

The boy admitted that he had used kerosene to aid his firesetting. The Reddton Public Library had undergone a paint-trim job in honor of Memorial Day. The kerosene, along with several cans of paint, were stored just beyond the Children's Section in the storeroom.

Damage was estimated at $40,000.

Miss Schuster is survived by a brother, Carl Schuster, of Reddton, and a sister, Mrs. Norma Arthur, of Selma, Missouri.

Too young to be charged with manslaughter, the boy was immediately turned over to juvenile authorities for detention, and eventual hearings in Children's Court.

Howard Berrey, father of the boy, refused to comment. His mother, Evelyn Berrey, was under medical treatment for shock.

Chapter Eighteen

REGINALD WHITTIER

It was Saturday evening. Reginald Whittier had arrived back home late yesterday, almost as Memorial Day was at a close. He had dragged himself up the stairs of Whittier's Wheel, exhausted from the drive, angry at himself for leaving Laura back in Montpelier without a word, and tired of being angry with himself.

He had come home where he was safe.

He had opened the door—left unlocked—and entered the dark living room of the apartment.

He had thought to say: *"Mother? Mother?"* but the dusty antique clock in the shop beneath him was striking midnight. He had smelled the odor of home, and for the first time since he had left this place, he had felt himself again.

Quietly, so as not to wake her, he had tiptoed past his mother's door to the bathroom.

Then he had heard the familiar tones, precise, slow, sing-song sounds of her voice late at night; Psalms.

"As for the children of men, they are but vanity; the children of men are deceitful; upon the weights, they are altogether lighter than vanity itself!"

"Mother?" he had said. "Mother?"

But he had known better than to expect a direct answer. He was home . . . with Miss Ella; back at the Wheel with his mother and her ways.

"Have I not remembered thee in my bed?" the voice continued from the bedroom of his mother, "and thought upon thee when I was waking? My soul hangeth upon thee."

"I'm home now, mother," he had said.

For an answer: "These also that seek the hurt of my soul, they shall go under the earth."

This morning, Reginald Whittier had gotten up at eight o'clock, the time he always got up when he was at home. He had walked into the living room and found his fresh orange juice, squeezed and waiting for him, in the same tall glass on the coffee table.

In the kitchen, his mother had been stirring her oatmeal on the stove.

"Mother?" he had said.

She had nodded at him without answering.

At eight-thirty, he had gone downstairs to the shop, turned the "Open" card to face the street side of the door, and walked back behind the counter . . . the way he always had when he was home.

So it had taken him this long to do what was expected of him; it had taken him from last evening to this evening to do it; and in between, there was the hell of self-hatred, and the anguish of Miss Ella's silence; and there was the bitter knowledge that he would do exactly what he *was* doing.

He knelt by her rocker in the living room of their apartment with his head in her lap, her lap muffling the sniffling, agonized sounds of his confession.

"And then?"

"I couldn't find a job. I was afraid no one would hire me."

"Of course you were. That's a normal fear, Reginald. Not everyone is patient with someone who stutters."

"She kept telling me I didn't."

"A woman like that will tell any lie to get what she wants, Reginald."

"We didn't have any television. It was just a bare room."

"Reginald, do you know I haven't watched *your* set once since you left? I bought it for you. With you gone, I wasn't interested."

"There were other things. Things I don't want to talk about."

"You'll have to get it all out of your system one day, but don't worry about it now, Reginald. You've purged yourself sufficiently for now."

"Thank you, mother."

"The marriage will be annulled."

"Shouldn't I try to call her? Send her some money, mother?"

"You'll have nothing more to do with that woman, Reginald!"

"She's a girl, mother. I'm older than she is."

"Just don't give her another thought. You're home, Reginald. You're where you belong."

"Yes, mother."

"We'll just carry on as though this hadn't happened."

"Thank you, mother. I'm sorry."

"I have ample forgiveness in my heart, Reginald. Ample forgiveness!" His mother smoothed his hair with her hand. "I can remember when you came home from the Boy Scout Jamboree, with that awful disease on your body. We can just thank God you don't have another disease."

"Yes, mother."

"Do you want to watch the television now, Reginald? The way we always do? Then I'll fix a little dinner."

"All right, mother."

"Chicken, and mashed potatoes, and fresh peas!" said Miss Ella. "Your favorites, Reginald. All your favorites." She took his hands from her lap and held them in her own. "When you were a little boy," she said, "I used to kiss these hands and tell you that God gave them to you for good deeds to be performed."

Reginald Whittier took his handkerchief from his trousers and blew his nose.

For a half-hour, he sat beside his mother watching the television set. It was a mystery story set in the South Seas. Miss Ella was audibly intrigued, but Reggie could not keep his mind on the screen. For one thing, he wished he dared walk into his bedroom and get the half-empty package of cigarettes from the bureau drawer. He wanted to smoke. Everything he seemed to want to do, and everything he seemed to say, reminded him of Laura. He remembered the way they had tumbled about on the floor —only yesterday—laughing and tickling one another, and kissing, like the married couple in that movie he and Laura had seen their first night in Montpelier. He thought of how Laura told him that she could cry when he was nice to her, and then he remembered the way *he* had cried in Mac's Diner, the way everyone had stared at him.

She was better off without him. He was sure of that. He might have done something terrible to her, something he couldn't help doing, just as he hadn't been able to keep from criticizing her all the time for practically nothing at all. Just as he had not been able to refrain from calling her Tobacco Road trash. She was better off with him gone . . . But she was pregnant, and she had told him she didn't want him to leave her.

"Isn't this exciting?" Miss Ella said.

"Yes, mother."

"I'm glad you're home. I knew you'd come home."

"Did you, mother?"

"I didn't have a real minute's worry, Reginald."

What about Laura? What about Laura right now, in the room by herself at the tourist home? She had been so sure everything would work out. She had never heard of a scrub. Of a *shrub,* she had, Reggie thought to himself, smiling, but not a scrub. Did she think he would be back "in a sec"? Was she washing out her underwear again and thinking Jeez, when will Reg be back? Reg. No one ever called him that before. Gloomy-ears, she called him. Gloomy-ears. And she had tickled him so hard he laughed until he was crying.

When his mother said, "Wasn't that interesting, Reginald?" he realized he had not heard or seen any of the television film.

"Yes, it was," he said.

"I knew that dark man in the Panama suit was the thief. I knew the moment I saw him. I'm going to start dinner while the news is on. That way we'll be all settled with our plates in front of us by the time Electric Theater starts."

"Yes, mother."

"Is it good to be back, Reginald?"

"I told you that it was, mother."

"You just forget all about it. We're going to have a very pleasant evening."

"I think I'll go to my room for a while, mother."

"Aren't you interested in the news?"

"I can hear it. I'll keep the door open."

"It was terrible about that quiz kid, wasn't it?"

"I don't believe he was spoofing," said Reggie, standing, stretching.

"No, I mean about the fire," said his mother. "He set fire to the library. Yesterday afternoon. Right in his home town, and the librarian was killed."

"Really?"

"It was in all the newspapers, Reginald. It came over the radio too."

"I didn't hear that."

"Oh, yes. He was angry because his parents had pushed him too much."

"I didn't hear that."

"It came over the radio. He confessed."

Reggie walked across the room to his bedroom.

"Aren't we glad we have all our arms and limbs, and we're safe in our own cozy home, Reginald?"

"Yes, mother."

"That makes the second Memorial Day weekend tragedy. There was that boy in upstate New York too."

"I read about that."

"That girl must have been some girl! Some nice girl, letting a boy take her out in the country that way, in the rain!"

"What's the rain got to do with it, mother?"

"I'm fixing all your favorites for dinner," said his mother. "Aren't you glad you're back?"

He did not answer her. If he were to walk into the bathroom, with the cigarettes in his trousers, his mother would never notice. He could smoke in there. There was a bottle of air-refresher in there, and he could spray some of it around to kill the odor. He opened his top bureau drawer to get the package of cigarettes.

Suddenly, his mother appeared in the doorway.

"I'm glad you're home, Reginald."

"You told me that, mother."

"I wouldn't have any other boy for a son. I'm glad you came to your senses."

"Thank you, mother."

"With children running around murdering and raping and setting fire, I'm glad you're safe and sound and back here where you belong."

"All right, mother. All right! We said we'd forget it!"

"Oh, I know there are things on your mind. Things you haven't told me, Reginald. You'll have to get it all out of your system, after dinner, when Mr. Danker comes."

"Mr. Danker?"

"You can have a long talk with him. I won't pay any attention. You and Mr. Danker can sit in a corner of the living room and have it all out."

"What's Mr. Danker got to do with anything, mother?"

"I understand you better than you think, Reginald. I know you want to get it out of your mind—all of it."

"I *said*, what's Mr. Danker got to do with it?"

"Now, we won't discuss it before dinner. You know how an argument before dinner can upset your digestion. You've always had a queasy stomach, even as a little boy."

"I don't want Mr. Danker to come here, mother. Ever!"

"He tried his best to keep you from running off with that woman! He told me all about it!"

"She's a girl. A kid! An eighteen-year-old kid!"

"She taught you to smoke, didn't she? She taught you to acquire *that* filthy habit too!"

"You took them, didn't you, mother?"

"Yes, I destroyed them. You needn't bother looking in your drawer for them, Reginald."

"I want them back!"

"Reginald, you're talking to your *mother!*"

"I want them back!" he said, walking toward her. "I want my cigarettes back!"

"I destroyed them!"

"I'll geh-geh-get them, I'll geh-geh—"

"What are you doing? Reginald Whittier, what are you picking up in your hands!"

"It's a ha-ha-ham-mer, mother."

"I know what it is! Put it down, right now," she said. "I'm your mother!"

"I know who you are," said Reginald Whittier, raising the kitchen hammer in the air, "Muh-muh-moth-er!"

EPILOGUE

EPILOGUE

Chapter Nineteen

BROCK BROWN
CHARLES BERRY
REGINALD WHITTIER

*(From the Labor Day issue
of a national news magazine)*

ALL SHOOK UP

Almost to no one's surprise, the past Memorial Day weekend was filled with tragedy characteristic of the holiday time. Among the statistics of automobile deaths, home accidents, drownings and racing-car crashes, there were three tragedies not quite as common to the normal long weekend—and yet, vaguely reminiscent of past Christmas, Easter, and Labor Day celebration periods, in this time of the youth gone cuckoo.

Manhattan psychiatrist Arnold Kurgler, commenting on the three murders committed by young people over the Decoration Day hiatus, said the reason for many such brutalities occurring on "special occasions" might well be attributed to too much family pressure.

"Children are usually underfoot more at such times," said the paunchy, balding authority, "and if they are not welcome, if they feel that they are in the way of the cocktail party, the barbecue, the napping father, or the sibling who wants the family car at the same time they do, the inhibited resentment is triggered, and mere impulses may become raging compulsions."

Manhattan Chief of Police Jack Graney chose

155

stronger language to explain the phenomenon of the rise in crime among youngsters during holidays.

"We've watched this thing for a long time," said cigar-smoking, hefty, tight-knuckled "Mutt" Graney, "and it all adds up to the fact that the kids are out to raise hell whenever there's a few days with nothing for them to do! We put extra men on to watch it, and we've been proven right. This last long weekend in New York City, there were no murders committed by kids, only four known thefts committed by criminals under 18, and very few acts of violence of any other kind. When you know there's going to be a rough time, you got to put on your gloves, stick in your mouthpiece, and go in fighting!"

Whatever the cause of juvenile crime, and if there is any consistency to its pattern during a vacation time, none of the youthful offenders of this past Memorial Day weekend were able to shed any light on the matter.

In Sykes, New York, handsome, immaculate 16-year-old Brock ("my mother's maiden name—she was a Brock") Brown was asked why he committed the rape-choke-knife murder of Caroline Bates, the same age. He gave the inarticulate, shoulder-shrugging answer almost any teen-ager gives for almost anything these days, from why he dances the fish, to why he leaves a girl's brutally stabbed body on a back-country road and goes home to change his clothes and watch television. His answer? "I was all shook up."

In Reddton, New Jersey, the parents of Charles (Chuckles) Berrey, poor loser on the Cash-Answer television quiz program, could think of no way to explain why their son set fire to the local library, causing the 59-year-old, white-haired librarian, Margaret Schuster, to die in the flames. They adamantly denied the rumor that their "Chuckles" had made the blaze out of anger at his failure to identify a zebra swallowtail butterfly, thereby losing $52,000 and allegedly inspiring his family's scorn.

The eight-year-old had little to add to his

parents' silence on the subject. His statement? "I'm sorry." His next thought. "I want my brother to have my knife collection. He doesn't live with my family. He lives in West Virginia."

The tall, stuttering, Vermont 19-year-old who beat his mother's head in with a hammer in the sleepy New England town of Auburn, Vermont, was more direct in his response to the question: "Why did you do it?" but was by far the least endearing of the three.

"She wouldn't give me back my cigarettes," he said, "so I picked up the hammer and hit her."

Brock Brown and hammer-killer Reginald Whittier were declared legally sane. Both will stand trial on charges of homicide. Quiz kid Berrey was released in his family's custody due to his age.

At the Memorial Day weekend's finish, the Eastern part of the nation, was almost as "shook up" by the shocking fact of these three sordid crimes as the "shook-up" generation itself.

THE END
of an Original Gold Medal Novel by
Vin Packer